Dear Glen & Anna,
Merry Christmas (2002)
With all our love,
Ru, Jim, Jacob, Dan & Harry.
X   X   xx   xx

New Fiction

MIXED BAG

Edited by

Heather Killingray

First published in Great Britain in 2002 by
NEW FICTION
Remus House,
Coltsfoot Drive,
Peterborough, PE2 9JX
Telephone (01733) 898101
Fax (01733) 313524

SB ISBN 1 85929 050 7

FOREWORD

When 'New Fiction' ceased publishing there was much wailing and gnashing of teeth, the showcase for the short story had offered an opportunity for practitioners of the craft to demonstrate their talent.

Phoenix-like from the ashes. 'New Fiction' has risen with the sole purpose of bringing forth new and exciting short stories from new and exciting writers.

The art of the short story writer has been practised from ancient days, with many gifted writers producing small, but hauntingly memorable stories that linger in the imagination.

I believe this selection of stories will leave echoes in your mind for many days. Read on and enjoy the pleasure of that most perfect form of literature, the short story.

Parvus Est Bellus.

CONTENTS

ASSUMPTIONS
Jillian Shields

The sun's light shone brightly in the clean window of the sky that morning. Industriously, she set off, the rhythmic tapping of her heels echoing around the deserted solitude of the street. Life seemed to have stopped - well, there weren't many people who chose to get up at daybreak. She thought of them all, lying listlessly in their beds, getting up at the alarm clock's command, having to hurry to work. She smiled contentedly, happy to be unique.

As she walked, the birds and trees seemed to appreciate the flutter of movement before the streets became crowded, when people could neither see, or would choose to ignore, the natural beauty of the town. She checked her watch; 6am - right on schedule. Like clockwork, her feet carried her lightly into the park. A far cry from the office, but a pleasant change from busy corridors, crimson faces and moaning lawyers. Still, in a strange way she liked it - notably more so with the arrival of a certain stranger with those swirling eyes, so deep you felt that if you dropped a stone into them it would never reach the bottom. But she wouldn't think about him anymore. It wasn't worth it with Maria there. Maria. How she envied *her*.

Maria was the Manager's secretary and it was more than obvious why she had been appointed to that position. Her mother was Italian and Maria seemed to have developed into a better version of her. She had the coal-black Italian hair, swirling in gentle waves, piled high upon her head. She always left a few tendrils loose to cascade around the flawless face in which she would twist her fingers if challenged or bored. Always, she wore exquisite tailoring, the best perfume and skirts of an apt length to show off her long, shapely legs to perfection.

Maria was always smiling. She would give her full attention to the speaker and would throw her head back to laugh, revealing a set of polished pearls that anyone would be proud to call teeth. Naturally, she had the attention of every man in the office, not least the handsome stranger newly arrived. Who could compete with her? Least of all a mousy-haired country girl with thick glasses and an overactive imagination. She sighed, sinking down onto a bench. Pleased, the ducks flocked to her feet for their daily feeding of fresh bread straight from the bakery.

'What can I do?' she demanded of her quacking companions. One waddled free to push its beak under her hand, as though for comfort. 'At least you understand!' she laughed, but nevertheless feeling better.

It was twenty minutes too late when Maria arrived at the office. Even so, she still made her arrival public; she could do it without even trying. Jane peered over her glasses at the air of silence but strayed back to the book on seeing it was only Maria. The handsome stranger's gaze lingered there, however, observing the sweet Italian perfume, drinking in the blazing beauty. Looking up again, Jane noticed Maria's air of innocence, masking the albeit intense glance in the stranger's direction. Flirting must be a natural gift, she concluded, retreating behind the glasses again and into thought.

She would think about many things while reading. She seemed to have a two-tier mind, taking in the book but thinking as well. Mind you, she'd much rather be able to flirt! To say that Jane was different was a somewhat understatement. She preferred her own company or that of animals and had no real friends - simply acquaintances at work who knew her as the 'mousy creature with the glasses'. As for her 'love-life', she'd never been close to anyone before. The only beings that truly loved her were her numerous pets. But she preferred it that way.

She enjoyed knowing that no-one could access her thoughts and hence her excessive imagination, which she relieved through writing poetry. No-one knew much about her and no-one had ever visited her home save one cousin - Emmeline - her only relative who called on Christmas Eve, probably out of obligation. It wasn't that she was unfriendly; simply shy and humble and hating to inflict her boring personality on anyone.

She was jolted back to the office by a pile of documents which landed noisily on her desk.
'Hey you! I want these typed - and now! You may only be a typist but that doesn't mean you can slack off and read books!'

'Yes Mr Thornton,' she replied meekly and the thick glasses seemed to focus her anger into a narrow beam which plunged into the Manager's scrawny back and followed as he exited the room. How she detested that man. He'd never liked her - the only woman he even *tried* to be pleasant to was Maria, and even then only because she was pretty. Life just wasn't fair. The sight of Maria herself approaching the desk didn't make her feel any better.

'Hi Jane. Listen, I'm really sorry about Scott, he's under a lot of pressure at the moment. Anyway, I just called to give you this.'

'This' was a leaflet about a staff party to be held on Saturday to celebrate 'Our New Partner' - better known as the handsome stranger in the firm.

'You'll be coming I hope.' Maria was concerned.

'Well, I suppose . . . '

'Great! I'll see you at seven-thirty!'

'Great' indeed! Jane was not a party person. She'd never drunk in her life and the only discos she'd attended were at secondary school. And what was she going to wear? She contemplated phoning Emmeline. A party! She'd rather stay at home and write poetry about the handsome stranger - much easier than facing him. But then a wave of anger stabbed her. To hell with it, she would take a chance! She had to make *some* change in her life!

That evening, she decided. It was time to get out of the mould - become better within herself. She confidently ascended the stairs and entered her 'perfect' room. That was part of the problem! She pulled a few clothes from the wardrobe and scattered a couple of shoes and scarves around. Perfect. Reaching above the wardrobe, she felt for the box. As her hands closed around it, she felt the same kind of apprehensive thrill known only once as a fourteen-year-old disobeying her parents. As she opened it, the faint, musty smell wandered to her nostrils and enhanced her delusion. She saw the cluster of pretty lipsticks and eyeshadows . . .and tweezers. 'No-one will laugh at me - I'll show them!' they seemed to shout.

Sitting in front of the mirror, she studied her face. Mousy, wiry hair, small eyes, caterpillar eyebrows. Was there potential? She had less than three days to find out. Grabbing the tweezers, she yanked out an offensive hair. It brought tears to her eyes but she was determined to get a good shape. Pluck, pluck, pluck. Wiping away the protesting tears, she looked at herself. What a difference! She looked almost passable! Gulping, she reached for the Yellow Pages and found the hairdresser's page.

'Yes, hello, I'd like to make an appointment for Saturday afternoon, please.'

It was done. She could feel a bit of that old stubbornness rising in her and her excitement grew like a nurtured seedling. She made three more appointments. All of Saturday morning would be spent with a beautician, facial for Thursday, optician's on Friday evening. Time to go shopping. As she walked along the High Street, a neon sign caught the corner of her eye. It was *Mulensa* the designer shop. Stopping, she allowed her head to follow her eyes. In the window was a black dress - long, with a slit up one side to the thigh, thin straps and little reddish sparkly bits all over it. It was very figure-hugging and expensive-looking, she thought as her eyes caught the six-hundred pounds price tag! With a surge of resolution she forced herself to go through the door.

'Can I help you Madam?' asked a slightly bemused sales assistant, not thinking much of the mousy, glasses-wearing young woman but fulfilling her obligations anyway.

'I'd like to try on the dress in the window, please.'

The assistant said nothing, her eyes more than averagely wide.

'Certainly.'

Finding the dress, she took Jane to the fitting room and swung open the door.

'Good luck Madam.'

'Thank you.'

Locking the door, Jane looked in awe at the wall-possessing mirror. She felt the dress, the material feeling silky and healing to her timid hands. It seemed to cry out to her to let it love her, nourish her skin. Slipping off her clothes, she carefully fitted herself into the heaven-made garment. Turning away from the mirror, she released her hair from its wiry prison and shook it around her face. Closing her eyes, she held her breath and turned around. Scared to open them, she forcibly flicked them open suddenly and studied the woman, yes woman, peering back at her. Although she looked hunched and shy, she was a beautiful woman. Pulling her back straight and her shoulders high, she admired the difference. In this dress she could rival even Maria!

She was wakened from fascination by a tap on the door.

'How is it, Madam?'

In reply, she pulled back the lock, opened the door and revealed the new Jane. The assistant's eyes widened again, though not with bemusement but with surprise.

'You look . . . absolutely beautiful! I've never seen anyone suit that dress so well. You *must* have it!'

'I think I will,' replied Jane.

'Of course you'll need shoes, a bag . . . what's the occasion?'

'Office party.' Jane stated this confidently now.

'I think you'll get promoted once your boss sees you in that!'

Jane smiled hopefully. Facial tomorrow!

The next day in work, Jane noticed a slight change in attitude towards her, particularly Maria who seemed to stare at her for a few minutes longer than usual. 'If this is what new eyebrows can do, what about the rest?' thought Jane, feeling excitement rise again.

Saturday morning. With half an hour to get to the salon, the optician's voice of the previous evening echoed back to her.

'Of course we can rid you of these glasses, and since it's urgent we'll drop your contacts off in an hour.'

Here they were. And she experienced sight truly - something unknown after her seventh birthday.

At the salon, Jane felt totally relaxed. As the beautician worked her magic, she visualised herself entering the hall. How they would look and stare in awe! She felt her joy mounting and found it almost difficult to answer the beautician's questions.

A beauty treatment and hair appointment later, a new woman had truly emerged. Following expert advice, red lipstick accentuated the newly blonde and feathered hair and generously outlined white teeth. As she slipped on the dress, the same confidence resumed. Even as she walked into the room later that evening, the confidence remained. Head held high, her non-obstructed eyes carefully placed the handsome stranger, who responded with a puzzled look. If she had known his thoughts, she would have changed her actions.

Gracefully lifting a champagne flute from a waiter's tray, she catwalked over to the handsome stranger's place at the bar.
'Hi,' she said softly.
'Hi there.' Strangely, his eyes seemed to hold a vague discord.
'You know me?' she quizzed, still not faltering.
The response was utterly unexpected. 'Thought I did.'

As her eyes widened, the stranger arose from his 'perch' and passed her to cross the room. Turning, puzzled, she spotted Maria smiling happily with a group of colleagues. Casually, the handsome stranger approached her, sliding his arms around her waist and kissing her cheek. Looking down, Jane saw the unmistakable flash of a ring. With a sickening realisation, she clutched her new-found friend, champagne, for comfort.

UNHOOKED
Ruth Richards

'Take him down.'
As the words echoed round the hushed courtroom, numbness overtook her. Her eyes drifted, bewildered, to the florid, bejowled face of the judge.
For a second his hooded, rheumy eyes caught hers, then moved disdainfully away. She could not drag her gaze from him as he began to stack and shuffle his papers, preparing to make his exit.
She knew his mind had already moved on, probably wondering what to have for his lunch. Billy, already a redundant memory that wouldn't resurface unless he saw him before him again. Just a morning's work.
She became vaguely aware of someone calling her name.
'Jo, come on love, I'll see if I can get you a visit.'
It was Betty, their solicitor's assistant. Jo allowed herself to be propelled to her feet by the gentle pressure on her arm. Her limbs felt as leaden and sluggish as her mind. As she looked wide-eyed into Betty's face, a single tear escaped and slid silently down her cheek. The life she carried in her womb fluttered, as though gently sensing her grief. She leant on Betty as she led her out into the foyer where she sat her down on one of the moulded plastic chairs.
Then she was alone. The sounds around her seemed muted, she felt disconnected, apart, a spectator. Shifting awkwardly in her seat, she tried to ease her swollen body into a more comfortable position. The baby thrashed its disapproval.
She leaned back and sighed, shutting her eyes to the glare of the strip lights. Instinctively she wrapped one hand protectively around her bump, and breathed deeply.
Her thoughts returned to Billy, wondering how he was reacting. His mouth was still hanging agape as they had led him away, she had seen the naked panic in his eyes. Then Betty returned, bringing Jo a much needed cup of strong black coffee.
'Thanks Betty,' she mumbled appreciatively.
'Are you alright, love?' Betty asked kindly.
'Yes, course I am,' Jo replied with a wan smile.
'Mr Bridges would like a quick word with you if you're up to it, love, then you can go down and see Billy for a few minutes.'

Jo turned to the heavily built, immaculately turned out man. It suddenly struck her as bizarre for him to be wearing a wig at a time like this.

He smiled woodenly, hardly disturbing his carefully trimmed salt and pepper beard. He began to explain to her about an appeal, how it would work and what their next step would be, but Jo found he couldn't apply herself to his words.

His voice seemed to become muffled and indistinct, her head was spinning slightly, and she wondered if she was going to be sick. She found herself staring at his perfectly manicured fingernails, hearing nothing that he said.

She gulped at her coffee in an attempt to revive herself and managed to hold on until the man had finished his monologue. Then it was over and he was reaching out to shake her hand. She took his hand and shook it feebly, a puzzled expression passed across his face, then he was gone.

She turned wearily to Betty.

'Can I see him now?'

By the time she was perching her bulk on the hard plastic stool, she was exhausted. She rolled herself a cigarette, figuring the baby would forgive her under the circumstances.

She stiffened as she heard the jangle of keys and the heavy metallic clunk of the door. Billy was led in and sat down opposite her. Her hand went involuntarily to the thick perspex that separated them.

He looked twitchy, his eyes darting nervously around. He looked in need of a hit. He had developed a serious habit in the six months he had been on remand. He had shrugged aside her fears, saying that heroin was a prison drug and he was only using for the duration. She'd made herself believe, but it had changed him already.

'Six years! You know what this means.' he blurted out.

Then before she had time to respond, 'It'll be another four years before they even consider me for parole. They'll ship me out, then how are you going to get to see me if I'm miles away?'

'Don't worry Billy, we'll sort something out . . . '

'What? How? Three visits a month . . . I'll never manage. What am I going to do for money? I won't even have any hash to sell. I'll go mad Jo, I can't do it, I'm sunk without your visits.' His voice rose, hysteria threatening.

'What am I going to do with nothing . . . ?'

Gradually his voice went the same way as the barristers, she was disconnected again. The realisation that he was thinking only of himself and his habit, sunk deadeningly into her.

The veil lifted and the illusions she had carefully woven to protect herself unravelled before her eyes. She had known for ages really, but had acknowledged only what she had wanted to see. His fear wasn't fuelled by any overwhelming concern or need for her, she had become a service to him, nothing more.

The baby twisted violently within her, its presence strangely disturbing, yet comforting. He had no concern for her or the baby, only himself. How could she have believed in him for so long?

The answer came, simultaneous with the question. She had been blinded by their lifestyle from the very beginning, deluded by the drugs and bewitched by the money. There was no reason to look any deeper, now she was seeing him, and the life they had shared, for what it really was, stripped of his money, power and drugs.

Now, instead of riding high with him, sharing his ego trip, she was washed up on the shore, forced to see the stark reality of it all, including him. She could see the twisted version of him minus his flash car and wads of cash. What good there was in him consumed by the heroin he was using to compensate himself for all he had lost. She couldn't bear it anymore.

She became aware that her limbs were moving, she was pulling herself to her feet, and turning away from him. She was dimly aware that he was no longer talking. She rang the bell and stood staring blankly at it while she waited for a jailer to let her out.

Her eyes flicked briefly towards Billy, whose hysteria had returned from a brief dumbfounded silence and reformed as anger. She was aware of his shouts and futile punches to the perspex, his face contorted by rage, a face she had only glimpsed before. She knew then that she was irretrievably lost to him.

As two officers attempted to restrain him, another led her from the room.

'Bitch, you bitch, where the hell do you think you're going?' he screamed at her back.

She felt something had reached its maximum tension, then snapped. No more did she feel the agonising pulling apart as she left him. There was nothing tangibly dragging her back to him, as they always had been before. She felt freed, unhooked, something deep within her had broken and drifted away.

'Wait until I get out, bitch,' was the last threat she heard, muffled by the thick metal doors that now separated them. She already knew that guilt and pity would overwhelm her at some point, but she knew now what she had to do for the baby and herself.

Her legs felt like water, her heart pounded in her throat. Somehow she kept upright and moving. She left the cells and climbed the ramp that led to the foyer and exit. She drifted unhearing and unseeing past the security guards, through the door and outside into the cold March air. She caught her breath as the clean, sharp air filled her lungs. Still trembling and willing each foot in front of the other, she made shakily for the car.

A DISORDERLY HOUSE
Anne Lavis

Yes she'd been rumbled alright, but who? Which one of those young things had been the Judas? She hurled the lump of cake into the middle of the lake where the ducks had gathered. Not fun loving Amber surely? Golden Tansy? No, and Molly definitely not. She hadn't given it much thought before now, strange that. Then there was Gretel, doubtful. Sonia or was it Tonia? Megan, yes Megan Morgan the pretty little Welsh girl. They never did see eye to eye, and wasn't it her who looked like the Cheshire cat when she heard that the Governor wanted a word. The Dreaded Pound, that's what the girls used to call him.

She'd never forget that Monday morning or was it Tuesday? Whatever. He was shuffling through some files. 'Take a seat,' he called over his shoulder. His office was small but not cramped, above him hung Gainsborough's Blue Boy and behind her an amateurish water-colour seascape. His desk was old and highly polished with a word processor still in its box and a packet of ham sandwiches on top, a bright orange leaflet said 'Don't Let Your Bindweed Become A Bind, Four Friendly Ways For Eradication'. She yawned loudly. 'Be with you in a moment.'

Her longest red nail was chipped, with outstretched fingers she began to examine the rest, suddenly the leather chair spun round to face her, oh God, quickly fumbling for her handkerchief she just about managed to stifle the giggle. For Mr P was short and squat with an anaemic bald head, bulbous nose, and rather large ear lobes. He began an immediate search of his drawers, 'Ahh here we are.' He produced a brown folder and pondered over the contents. 'Juveniles' he muttered and ran the back of his hand slowly across the paper as if ironing out a stubborn crease.

When he looked up she was smiling widely at him. 'Forgive me Madam but I fail to see what's so amusing.' She bit her bottom lip, his only redeeming feature was a stunning pair of azure blue eyes, they fell onto the page. 'So here we have it.' His finger stabbed at the typing, names, dates, times, 'all the details in fact of your disorderly house, have you anything to say Madam?' The look was confrontational. Yes of course she had, but then, on the other hand some things were better left unsaid. She opened her mouth to speak. 'Ms Penelope Primm.' He scratched his left ear lobe. 'Rather an unfortunate name given the circumstances,' he said smugly. Penny wise, pound foolish, the old adage sprang from nowhere, but Christ she couldn't afford to antagonise the man further.

'Sir,' she wondered if politeness would help her case, 'as I'm sure you're aware these are liberated times in which we live, now if I might explain a few things to you, Sir.'

'Carry on.' He sank back into the black leather, his legs dangling over the edge of the chair. A loud knock was followed by the head of a good looking youth who gave her a knowing smile.

'He's arrived Sir.'

'Sorry.'

'Mr Swift, he's just flown in.'

'Oh good, tell him I'll be right there.'

'As I was saying.'

He returned the folder to its drawer, 'I'm afraid Madam this will have to wait.' He checked his watch thoughtfully and said, 'Shouldn't take too long, if you would care to wait in reception I'll be with you as soon as possible.' Then hurried off.

A free drinks machine stood in the corner with red instructions, 'For Staff Only'. Three coffees and half an hour later she'd had enough and slammed the door behind her.

The moorhens didn't show much interest in the stale breadcrumbs so she tossed them to the advancing coot. Up went the man's umbrella, the girl sheltered beneath the sapling.

A lone figure across the lake seemed oblivious to the short sharp shower. She peered hard, it was her, she'd let her hair go grey and now she wore glasses but it was her alright.

'Do you come here often?'

'No, not really.' She turned to face an attractive blonde with a light golden tan, scarlet T-shirt, and tight blue jeans.

'Don't remember me, do you Penny?'

Her face crumpled, 'No but I feel I should, give me a minute.' She searched her brain, 'Is it? It is, Marilyn Reynolds.'

'That's it, been a long time.'

'Yes it has, come and sit down,' she patted the park bench, 'and tell me all about yourself.'

'Well, do you know The Body Beautiful?'

'Yes.'

'It's mine.'

'Really, how lovely.'

'Yes and Pete and I.'

'Your husband?'

'Partner, we're planning to open another one soon, a bigger place in Island Gardens.'

'I always knew you'd go a long way.'

'So what do you do now Penny?'

'I help Petal twice a week, little florist on East Street, it helps me fill the gap.' She looked thoughtful. 'He's such a sweet boy.'

'Did you know it was Megan that blew the whistle?'

'Yes I realise that now.'

'She kept a diary, then one day she showed it to, now what was his name?'

'Pound, funny thing is I've been thinking about him.'

'Things weren't the same after you left.'

'Yes well,' she shrugged, 'do you keep in touch with the others?'

'No, not any more, oh except for Barbie and Sindy that is.'

'The Twins.'

The young couple walked slowly past, hand in hand, she smiled, he half turned and gave Marilyn a crafty wink.

'They're nurses now,' she said. 'They drink in the Elephant's Trunk at weekends, do you know it?'

'Yes, it's not far from me.'

'Well why don't you pop in Saturday night, the girls would love to see you, look I have to be going now Penny, mustn't keep the clients waiting, until Saturday then.'

'Yes I'm looking forward to it already Marilyn.'

Above the buzz of conversations she heard their hearty laughs, the twins hadn't changed at all.

'Let me look at you.' Barbie held her at arms length, pulled her to her ample chest then hugged her. 'Lovely to see you Penny, how are you?'

'I'm fine thanks and you both look well.'

'You left so suddenly, early retirement they said.'

'I had no choice.'

'We were a difficult lot, weren't we?'

'You were a challenge and I enjoyed every minute.'

Marilyn sipped her white wine.

'She's singing your favourite song Penny.'

Sindy raised her pint glass, 'I'd like to propose a toast, to Penelope, wife of Odysseus.'

'Mother of Telemachus,' quipped her twin.

'To Penny Primm our unconventional Tudor House teacher without whom the classics would have been so very, very boring.'

'Cheers Penny,' they chimed.

She smiled, and while Shirley Bassey sang about her life she brushed away a tiny nostalgic tear.

SOMEONE SPECIAL
Grace Whyte

'Mummy . . . Mummy . . .Oh! Daddy. Help . . . Help!' Lauren's blood-curdling screams shattered the velvet calm of the summer night sending Magic, the cat, under the hall table.

Barry, the first to wake, sat bolt upright and flinging the bedclothes to the bottom of the bed uncovered his shivering wife, Sara.

'Not again,' she moaned, 'this is the third time this week.' Now fully awake and trembling with the shock of such a rude awakening she made for the door, fast on the heels of her anxious husband.

They arrived at Lauren's bedroom door together and found the six year old shaking like a leaf and soaked in perspiration, her short, black hair standing on end in spiky disorder, eyes wide and staring.

She was speechless.

Something was certainly worrying the child, no sign of trouble during the day but the nightmares were creating problems for the whole family. Lack of sleep causes lost appetite and creates frayed nerves.

When the concerned parents had calmed Lauren and laid her to rest they went downstairs for a hot drink. Sara, small and dark, looking so much like her daughter, placed a pan of milk on the stove and wrapping her arms round her slim body shivered as she waited for the milk to heat.

Barry stood in the doorway watching in a helpless sort of way while running his hand round the fair stubble on his chin and leaned against the door frame.

'Something has to be done.'
'What? . . . Just tell me what and I will do it, anything to stop these sleepless nights. They are playing havoc with Lauren's schooling and she is changing from a happy, little soul into a whinging brat. She does not remember a thing the next day,' Sara paused in the act of filling two cups with the hot milk. 'I suppose that is just as well really or I think she would have mental problems, as it is she is just listless.'

The couple sipped their hot drinks in silence while Barry pondered, or at least appeared to and they trudged back to bed. He liked to think he made the decisions, in actual fact it was Sara who did but she had to give him time to consider the facts, he hated to be rushed.

Life went on, Lauren's nightmares subsided and were gradually forgotten.

'Wait for me . . Do wait Thomas!' Annie puffed and panted behind her brother as she toiled up the hill, hitching her heavy petticoats up in a most unladylike way. Her dainty, lace cap slipping over one ear as she sank on to the grass beneath the shade of the towering tree.

Thomas was already lying on his back gazing up at the lattice of leaves above his head. Cap tilted over his eyes, breeched legs crossed nonchalantly, he looked as if he had been there for hours. He chewed a blade of grass and spoke to the air above his head.

'This tree has got to come down.'

Annie paused in the act of pulling the wool together round a gaping hole in her stocking.

'No . . . Why? It is not harming anyone and the shade is so good on a hot day.'
'Aye it is, but the landlord wants to make a track and said the tree had to come down.'

Standing up Thomas gazed at the view of fields and villages stretching like a patchwork quilt before his eyes. Each time he looked at this view the villages seemed to grow larger, the rows of houses spreading like the stealthy fingers on a great hand, grasping the countryside in its hungry grip. Now when he thought about it, it was like the giant octopus which wrapped its tentacles round the men who were unlucky enough to fall into the sea. This was one of the stories his grandpa had told him. A sea-going captain, he had some very strange tales to relate.

'Grandpa says this tree is a living, breathing thing . . . It talks to other trees . . . And feels things like pain, and when animals live in its trunks it welcomes some and rejects others.'

Annie stood up and whacked the tree with a stick. 'I cannot hear anything.' She gazed up at the solid mass twisting round towards the canopy of leaves above her head. Did it tremble? She took another hasty look, no it was only the breeze whispering caressingly through the foliage.

It was a strange looking tree, more like several trees twisted together almost as if they were holding each other, reaching up into the blue haze and escape.

'Grandpa says this tree is as old as time and since the beginning of time has grown and grown, outliving many generations of people.'

Annie gave the tree another hefty blow. 'Alright I do not want to hear any more about his silly tree.' She brushed the grass off her skirt. 'Race you . . .' And away she went down the hill, shawl flapping around her heels as she trailed it behind her. Thomas followed and the tree shook with rage; perhaps it was the wind increasing velocity.

The landlord did try to remove the tree but after the death of one man and two men badly injured, due to falling branches, he had to give up. He did not want to be supporting their families for the rest of their lives so compromised by having the branches savagely cut back.

Barry and Sara thought they had nursed Lauren through the nightmare stage until she reached the age of twelve years and then they started again, much worse than they had ever been previously. Now she was older she could relate a little more to her parents the terror of her dreams.

The terrible screams seemed to penetrate into her very soul, tingling along her nerve ends, setting her whole being burning with the agony of the screaming creature. For no human could produce such sounds.

She was always walking in her nightmares, on and on following the tortured cries. She had to find out where they were coming from but as the sound became deafening she walked with her hands clamped over her ears. Until she saw it. The poor, poor tree twisting and writhing, stretching its branches towards her pleading for help. But she could not do anything and turning to run, stumbled over the broken branches the woodsman had left to be collected the next day. The sap running out of the sawn wood like blood, for in her nightmare it was red and thick, pulsating with life.

Oh! The wickedness of the destruction.

Lauren ran and ran, hands over ears, tears streaming down her face. And that is how her parents found her night after night and her health began to suffer. She could not eat and was so tired, just wanted to sleep and then the torture would start all over again.

Sam and Barry agreed their daughter would have to stay off school and Sara took her for walks on Hampstead Heath. They could see a long way over the suburbs of the city, no longer villages, instead, streets upon streets flanked by trees. Gradually as Lauren became stronger their walks became longer. On such a day Magic, the cat, followed them and while Sara stopped to scold and pick the animal up, Lauren walked on.

Sara caught her up to find her standing transfixed in front of a group of people. They were New Age folk and were busy packing up a tent and cooking utensils, singing happily while they did so. Lauren was not looking at them, she was gazing past them at the tree towering above their heads, at least it was only the trunk of a tree. Completely shorn of its leaves it stood, its solid trunk twisting round and round like several trees holding each other up in their agony.

Lauren fainted.

The New Age folk were very kind and Sara found herself telling an intense, young woman about Lauren's nightmare. The woman did not laugh, she was serious and when Sara had finished telling of her worries to Elly, for this was the listener's name Elly passed her a mug of tea and said, 'Go home, your daughter will be fine now the operation is over. You see after all the hacking and cutting the tree still lives. Thanks to our vigil the woodsman has spared it and pruned it right back instead.' She pointed to the side of the tree, 'There are fresh shoots growing again.' Elly gently took hold of Sara's arm. 'Take great care of you daughter, she is special, just as my seafaring ancestor was. He passed down stories to my great uncle Thomas and described this tree so we knew where and when help was needed.' She patted the tree, 'It is safe for a long time to come.'

The tree sighed . . . or perhaps it was the wind caressing the cluster of leaves on its side.

THE EARLY CONNECTION
T Daley

The doctor heaved a sigh of relief as he entered the front door of his house. Home at last, he thought. God I am so tired. He had been called out the last ten consecutive nights on emergency calls, so between his interrupted nights of sleep and his extremely busy days, he was feeling worn out and the resultant irritability was starting to show, especially in the relationship with his wife.

She was a young wife and mother of a two month old baby girl, she also was feeling very tired these days, what with being a housewife, mother, part-time doctor's secretary and general handy woman. Her days were long and full of work but she knew how keen her husband was to make a success of this, his first practice on his own and also to be accepted by the local people.

They had only moved into the village about four months ago and had not, as yet, broken down the resistance of the villagers and patients from the surrounding area. They still clung to the advice and treatment of the previous doctor who had held the practice for over fifty years, small wonder that the villagers were reluctant to ignore the old doctor now that he had retired, and were even more reluctant to consult 'that new young doctor'.

But tonight was a special night. It was the young couple's third wedding anniversary. The wife had been working hard all day preparing and cooking a special meal for the evening. The scene was set, the dining table was laid out perfectly, candles flickered and the lights were mirrored in the silverware laid out. A beautiful display of flowers adorned the centre of the table. The doctor entered the room and saw the lovely setting. He was greatly affected and stood still for some time examining the scene and noticing all the things that his wife had done to make this a special evening. His heart was full of love and gratitude and he vowed to himself he would make every effort to control his behaviour in future. Just then his wife entered the room.

'For you darling,' he said handing her a bouquet of roses and a package, and added, 'you look lovely.'

His wife had made a special effort in her appearance. She wore the dress she knew was his favourite, her hair was carefully groomed, her perfume was subtle but noticeable. She wore earrings, necklace and bracelet and the stones caught the candlelight.

'You remembered,' she said handing him a beautifully wrapped box tied with a silk ribbon and added, 'thank you darling.'

'Of course,' he said. 'I'll never forget this day, I'm sorry I have been a bit touchy lately but I have been so tired and I want so much for us to be accepted here.'

'I know,' she said. 'I understand, but forget about work for a while, the baby's sleeping, so let's have a lovely meal, everything is ready.

They kissed and opened their gifts with exclamations of delight and then sat down to eat. The meal was delicious, the wine was good, the music was soft and sentimental and gradually the both began to relax and enjoy themselves. Later they drank coffee in front of the fire and talked softly such as they had not done for years, each one apologising for their behaviour and vowing eternal love. Then they danced until they were tired and went to bed.

It was just 2.10am when the telephone jangle cut through the doctor's dream like a sharp knife. Instantly the doctor was awake and answered it. Yes it was Mrs Hopkins, could the doctor come and treat her leg. She was in agony. Of course. He looked down at his beautiful wife lying there and kissed her gently on the cheek, but she did not stir. He groaned as he heard the rain beating on the window and the howling of the wind, and at the thought of turning out again. However, he quickly dressed, grabbed his medical bag and left.

Fortunately the patient, Mrs Hopkins, lived only ten minutes away and was soon there, comforting her and giving her a pain killing injection. She thanked him profusely, 'Oh doctor,' she said, 'thank you for coming. I know some of the people in the village have been against you, but I will tell them all how good you have been.'

The doctor smiled and said, 'It's alright Mrs Hopkins, phone me if you get any more pain and goodnight.' Then he left.

It was about a quarter to four as he undressed and got back into bed and he sighed blissfully as he sank into the warm bedclothes. The baby's cry immediately woke the mother, in an instant she was wide awake and got out of bed, she put the light on and saw the time was nearly 4.30am, she looked down at her husband who was fast asleep. How tired he looks she thought as she bent her head to kiss him. Then she hurried to the nursery and picked up the baby from the cot. She soon prepared a feed and fed the baby and after changing her the baby was content and soon fell asleep again. The mother was pleased that it had not taken long, some nights or mornings she had spent hours with the baby. She noticed it was nearly 5.30am when she gratefully got back into bed.

In the morning, the sun was shining as they both got up to start a new day and a new beginning to their marriage and a new start in their village life. It was at the breakfast table that her husband said to his wife, 'Did you have a nice sleep last night? You were looking lovely when I went out.'

'What! You went out last night,' said the wife incredulously, 'and I never heard the telephone ring at all, besides you were fast asleep when the baby cried and I got out to see to her and I thought you were having a nice uninterrupted sleep.'

'Well, I never heard the baby cry,' said the doctor. 'Isn't it strange?'

Who can explain why the doctor hears the phone and not the baby and the mother hears the baby and not the phone?

SKYRANGER
Richard Langford

'Inspector Ferrino!' A young police officer burst into the central office at police headquarters in Calgary, Canada.

'What is it?' asked the dark, thick-set man seated behind the desk. He was a tough Italian who did not suffer fools gladly.

'It's the killer-Frank Rockwell - he has escaped from the State Penitentiary and he is right overhead in a helicopter, Sir!' exclaimed the officer.

Ferrino's eyes widened; he jumped up from the desk.

'What happened?' he asked, walking towards the high, sunlit windows of the tower block.

'He is holding a helicopter pilot at gunpoint,' replied the young officer quickly.

'What's his name?' replied Ferrino, scanning the bright, blue sky above the city.

'Harry Angelo,' replied the young man, 'he was taking a television cameraman up to the prison and they had just touched down outside the yard when Rockwell climbed the fence and dived into the chopper.'

'I see,' replied Ferrino.

Above, a small helicopter with a brightly lit perspex canopy was circling.

'He wants to speak to you Sir,' said the younger officer.

'Okay, hand me the microphone,' frowned Ferrino.

'Is that you, cop?' snarled the craggy-faced, ageing killer in the prison uniform, high above.

'Yes, this is Ferrino,' replied the man calmly. 'what can I do for you, Rockwell?'

'I want one hundred thousand dollars in cash and a plane to fly me out of the country.' replied Rockwell,'Get the whole thing together on the airstrip at Salt Lake City or the guy in the chopper here gets it.'

Ferrino thought quickly; the lout had killed a dozen men, including police officers.

'Okay, cool it Rockwell,' he said, 'you have a deal.'

Salt Lake City rose out of the distant haze, its buildings lay like a pile of children's blocks, thrown down upon a pale grey carpet of inestimable width.

'We made it, Harry,' smiled Rockwell, his little green eyes shining wickedly down.

'You are never going to make it, Rockwell,' Harry snapped back, 'the best thing you can do is give yourself up the moment we land.' Rockwell laughed.

'Sure Harry, sure, the cops will give me a great welcome now I've put some of their buddies in the ground - you dumb b*****d! Do you think I'm crazy or something?'

Harry did not reply. The young, fair-haired pilot and private detective kept silent.

'Turn on your radio,' snapped Rockwell as the chopper burned in over the city, 'where is the airport in this place?' Harry indicated a long, flat strip of land about a mile ahead of them. Already a string of cars lined the runway. Police were swarming around the airport buildings like ants. A car pulled away from the edge of the tarmac, racing back towards the city, lights flashing. A white jet aircraft stood out on the runway, the sun glinting on its polished canopy. The radio in the chopper crackled;

'Salt Lake City, this is Harry Angelo, do you read me?' There was a brief pause then a voice crackled back,

'We read you, Angelo,'

'Do you have details of the situation?' asked Harry, anticipating the answer.

Down below, frenzied activity on the tarmac made it obvious that everyone at the airport knew all about the killer at his side.

'Affirmative - you are clear to land,' came the reply. Harry turned to face Rockwell.

'What do you plan to do with me?' he asked. Rockwell grinned wickedly.

'Well Harry,' he said, 'over the past few hours you have kept telling me how important it is that I should keep you alive.'

'So? It was the truth wasn't it?' frowned Harry.

'It sure was,' replied Rockwell, 'but now, buddy, you have outlived your usefulness. Once I reach that plane down below, you are going to go the same way as all the rest - and you know something? I think I'm going to enjoy putting a bullet in your back - you're really beginning to get to me.'

'Oh no,' thought Harry 'It's not going to be that easy.'

The helicopter came in to land. Rockwell pushed Harry Angelo out. They made for the plane. There was a movement within the aircraft near the small flight of steps which ran up to the doorway.

'Damn you double-crossing b*****ds!' yelled Rockwell, 'I didn't think you'd be fool enough to try this!'

There was a rapid exchange of gunfire on the tarmac. The police dived for cover, but in seconds Rockwell had leapt inside the fuselage and blown them apart. Blood splattered the walls of the cabin as the convict swung round, blasting holes through the sides of the jet. Harry dropped down to the side of the stairway and rolled beneath the aircraft, taking shelter behind one of the large wheels of the plane. A police marksman's bullet missed its furious target by inches as Rockwell lurched out of the doorway in a lethal rage. He spun round, firing to right and left, then jumped from the stairway as bullets tore into it. He ducked under the nose of the jet, putting it between himself and the police.

'Hold your fire!' yelled Ferrino, 'If that plane goes up they will both die out there!'

A police motorcyclist suddenly took the law into his own hands. Ignoring Ferrino's orders, he kicked the bike to life and sped out over the tarmac.

'What the hell is that man doing?' yelled Ferrino. The motorcyclist leapt from his machine with the intention of taking Rockwell out with one carefully aimed shot. As he hit the surface of the airstrip, flat on the ground, his bike toppled behind him, pinning him beneath it.

Rockwell dived behind the plane. The motorcyclist's shot flew far wide of the man and soon Rockwell added another name to his list. The police rider lay dead beneath his spluttering machine.

Rockwell saw his chance. He raced towards the bike, lying on its side on the runway.

'Take him!' yelled Ferrino. Bullets peppered the tarmac around the running killer.

'Why don't they hit him?' gasped Harry Angelo, still crouched by the wheel of the jet. Rockwell seemed to be indestructible. Diving and weaving, he dodged across the airstrip to the police motorcycle. Strong hands hauled it upright. In seconds he was speeding off along the runway, lurching from side to side to avoid the police bullets.

Ferrino yelled furiously, 'Take that man out - can't any of you shoot straight?' Rockwell scorched away from the airport buildings, heading for the gates of the airport. In seconds he had passed through them and roared away into the busy streets of the city. Harry leapt to his feet and ran back to the chopper. It sang into the air, circled the airfield, then spun away in pursuit of the crazed killer below.

'Get after that gunman!' Ferrino's voice was furious and harsh, 'Why the hell did you let him get away!' He slammed his car into gear and spun the wheel angrily. 'Rockwell is going out of his mind,' he snapped, 'while that man is loose no one in this city is safe.'

Cars roared after the motorcycle, sirens howling away across the airfield towards the city beyond.

Rockwell gripped the motorcycle furiously in his iron fists. The police were not going to take him without a fight. His rifle slung over his shoulder, he swung the motorcycle through the streets of the city like a madman. Horns blared about him. Rockwell began screaming like a lunatic.

'Look out lady! The devil is coming after you! I'm the devil, lady! Better run back to your church!'

Pedestrians scattered as the motorcycle, bearing its crazed rider, swung round onto a broad thoroughfare. Up ahead a high church building towered over the street. With a furious frown, Rockwell uttered a foul oath, then opened the throttle wide and roared away down the centre of the busy main road. Cars swerved to avoid the oncoming motorcycle. Gradually it increased in speed until it hurtled like a bullet towards the church at the end of the street.

'What the hell is he doing?' yelled Ferrino.

High up above, Harry Angelo watched in amazement. Driving like a man possessed, Rockwell mounted the pavement in front of the church and leapt the bike up the wide steps as if they did not exist. He was aiming directly at the main doors of the church.
'He'll kill himself!' yelled a man on the street.

The church doors thundered inward. Breaking glass showered away across the polished floor. The motorcycle roared down the centre aisle of the empty church, leaving shattered coloured glass and broken wood in its wake. It smashed against the communion rail, hurling its rider to the floor of the church. He leapt up, clutching his rifle.

High above the building, Harry was beginning his descent towards the flat roof of the high, grey stone building. Ferrino and his men leapt in through the shattered doors of the church. Shots echoed through the building. The police dropped to the floor behind the long rows of pews. Rockwell was blasting away furiously back up the centre aisle towards them.
'Let's get this b*****d!' snarled Ferrino angrily, coloured glass crunching beneath his shoes.

Rockwell looked about desperately for a way to escape the gradually increasing numbers of police who were beginning to surround the building. To his right a great organ stood, its pipes reaching upwards into the darkness. In seconds, Rockwell had leapt onto it, running upwards angrily, while Ferrino's men raced forward, firing shot after shot towards the frantic figure as he wound he way up towards the roof.

Harry Angelo stood on the flat surface above the oncoming killer. Suddenly, a wooden door burst open on the roof of the church. Harry heard gunfire.
'Well look who's here!' yelled Rockwell grimly. He seemed almost insane, eyes wide with confusion and rage. He turned and fired two shotgun blasts back down the spiral staircase.
'Get down!' yelled Ferrino. His men dropped to their knees on the stairway. In seconds Harry leapt upon the gunman, grasping at his rifle.
'I told you I would take you out Rockwell!' he yelled furiously.
'You stupid b*****d!' yelled back the killer, 'You're a walking dead man!'

They wrestled with the rifle, staggering across the church roof. Harry missed his footing and fell back onto the cold brickwork. Rockwell snatched away the rifle and turned it towards his attacker. Stunned by the fall, Harry gazed up at the figure before him. Slowly, the killer removed something from beneath his jacket. Harry gazed at it; it was a heavy brass candlestick holding a long candle. He had snatched it up in the church below.

Ferrino and his men were poised in the stairway, gazing out onto the roof.

'Keep back, cop! B*****d!' screamed Rockwell furiously. He turned back to Harry Angelo. The killer's face was a hideous mask of hatred. He pushed Harry towards the edge of the roof.

'Do you know your Bible, Harry boy?' he yelled. Harry did not answer the crazed killer with the long, brass candlestick.

'Remember the temptations of Christ, do you? How he was tempted to throw himself down from the roof of the temple - do you remember that one, Harry?' Harry nodded slowly. Rockwell stood close to him, pointing the barrel of the shotgun at his head.

'That was the devil who tempted him Harry - the devil himself and that's who I am - the devil himself!'

Rockwell had cracked.

'Last time the devil got beat, but this time it's going to be different! This time it's the good guy who's going to fall!' He held out the candlestick.

'Light it, Angelo, light it and then bow down before me.' Harry glared at him.

'I'll never bow down before you, you murdering scum!' He spat.

'Do it!' Rockwell's eyes were wild and blazing like fire before him.

'Worship me Harry, do it!'

'What the hell is going on up there?' said Ferrino. A uniformed officer turned back to face him.

'It's that guy Angelo, Sir - it looks like Rockwell is making him kneel down on the roof with a candlestick before him.'

'He's crazy!' snarled Ferrino, 'Completely crazy!'

Harry knelt on the rooftop holding the long, brass candlestick. He gazed down the barrel of Rockwell's shotgun. He lit the candle, protecting it from the wind with his cupped hand. He had noticed something, kneeling there beside Rockwell; an unmistakable odour could just be detected.

'Behold your king!' cried Rockwell. He raised his arms in triumph. The next second Harry had thrust the candle against his clothing. There was a great blast of flame. Rockwell became a blazing torch on the church roof. He staggered to one side, the rifle fell from his grasp.

'What is it? What is it?' he screamed,

'It hurts, oh God it hurts, it's burning! Help me!' he screamed in anguish, 'Help me!'

'I'll help you!' bellowed Harry Angelo.

He snatched up Rockwell's rifle. Two shotgun blasts smashed into the killer's face. He toppled backwards, then fell like a burning fireball down, down, into the street below.

The police raced out onto the rooftop. Harry sat back near his chopper, holding the rifle.

'Angelo - are you okay?' Ferrino leapt down beside him, 'Are you wounded?'

'No,' said Harry slowly, 'I'm fine, just fine.' Ferrino gazed down into the street where the body of Rockwell lay, a charred mass among the multitudes below.

'What - what happened?' he asked, turning back, 'Was it an act of God or something?'

'No,' said Harry, 'not this time.'

'What was it?' asked Ferrino.

'Petrol,' replied Harry, laying down the rifle. 'It was all over his clothes.'

'How did that happen?' asked Ferrino.

'Back at the airport when he stole the bike - it fell over on the airstrip, the petrol cap came off, it poured all over the bike. I saw it from beneath the plane. When he rode it through town the stuff saturated his clothes.'

'You touched them with the candle and that was it.'

'That's it,' said Harry. Ferrino looked around the skyline of the city.

'Well I'll be damned,' he said.

'No,' replied Harry - 'but he will.' He nodded down towards the street.

The two men descended into the church below.

'You're a private detective, right? From Vancouver?' said Ferrino.

'That's right,' said Harry. As he stood before the broken doors of the church, he realised for the first time in his life that he had the guts to make a go of it.

'Well nice going, kid,' said Ferrino. 'when I saw that guy go up in flames like that I knew that someone up there must like you.'

'Yeah,' replied Harry as they stepped through the debris, 'I think you're right.'

A CHRISTMAS GIFT, UNWRAPPED
G Hunter Smith

The two almost identical men stood on the snow-covered drive beside the younger man's car. The obvious differences between them were their ages and the fact that the elder one carried more weight around his middle.

'Thanks for giving me a bed for the night, Dad,'

'It was a pleasure having you here David, and I want to thank you for being so understanding. When you arrived out of the blue last night' David paused, looking hard at his new found son's face. Then the words poured out. 'I thought you were going to strike me, in which case we should have finished up with a fist fight. I'm very proud of you, you handled a tragic story very well under the circumstances.'

The younger man grinned easily. 'You certainly gave me a lot to think about, and I'm beginning to understand the dilemma you faced. Though I don't know what mother will make of it.'

'How is she?' David gasped, feeling the old familiar surge of excitement at the mention of her. 'You didn't talk about her last night. Is she well? How does she look?'

'Sorry Dad. I'm under strict instruction not to tell you anything about her. That was the condition she laid down in exchange for your address when I insisted that I wanted to meet you. Dammit Dad, I didn't even know that you were alive until a couple of weeks ago, and she told me that under no circumstances was I to divulge her address or telephone number. Look at it from her point of view. For over forty years she's hated even the very thought of you for abandoning her when she was pregnant. When I get home and explain it as you told it to me, well, we'll have to wait and see. She may relent, but I wouldn't hold my breath if I were you. Now I must go, it's a long drive.' He glanced around the snow-covered drive and garden and grinned again as they shook hands, before he climbed easily into the car. 'And if the roads are like this, it could be interesting.'

'Traffic should be light at this time of morning and it is Christmas Day.' David explained needlessly. The door closed as the car pulled away.

Suddenly, David had the strangest feeling. He was sure that his only link with the past had just been broken. Tears pricked at his eyes as he stuffed his cold hands into his trouser pockets, and stood watching the rear of the car as it moved slowly down the drive and turned onto the main road. Then sadly he turned and entered the lonely house, forcefully closing the front door behind him as though to shut out the memories. It didn't work.

With dragging footsteps, he walked along the passage and entered the lounge, not seeing the brightly decorated tree or the roaring fire in the hearth. Aimlessly, he wandered across and stood with his back to the fire, warming himself. His mind a madhouse of conflicting, jumbled thoughts. One thing singled itself out for attention. 'My son,' he murmured to the room. 'my son, David!' Another thought pushed forward.

He felt a moment of panic as he remembered his family. 'My God?' he gasped aloud. 'What can I say to Richard? How will he take it, suddenly finding out that he has a half brother. What will his wife say? Will the grandchildren like having a new uncle dropped on them?'

Doubts and uncertainty crowded into his mind and caused further agitation among the already chaotic jumble surging round and round.

He ambled across to the drinks cabinet and poured a healthy shot of ten year old malt whisky into a tumbler. Mindlessly he tossed it straight back. The fiery spirit burned into the lining of his stomach and seemed to jolt his overcrowded brain. He suddenly felt that he should have been more positive all those years ago. He should have told Cathy about Jenny, and Jenny about Cathy instead of trying to protect them both by keeping silent.

Without warning the words of an old song manifested themselves. He remembered the title, *The Sound Of Silence*. He spoke the words.
'People speaking without talking. People listening without hearing.'
The great revelation burst inside his head, as hot, stinging tears filled his eyes. That's what I've been guilty of all my life. Speaking about things that don't matter, but not talking clearly and fully explaining the meaning of what I did say when it was important, and being guilty of not listening enough. Almost being selective in what I wanted to hear.
'My God,' he groaned as he slumped into his favourite chair, wiped away the tears with the back of his hands and clasped his spinning,

throbbing head in his hands. 'what have I done?' He leaned back in the chair, closed his eyes and allowed his thoughts to drift.

David strode purposefully across the carpeted room and snatched up the telephone. He had finally made a decision and the die was cast. He was determined to find her. Quickly tapping out the numbers that he had selected from the Yellow Pages, he waited impatiently, fingers of his left hand drumming on the polished table top. Eventually a female voiced purred,

'Ajax Investigations, how can I help you?'

'My name is David Fox. Do you think that you can trace someone that I haven't seen in over forty years?'

'We can try Sir, but you must realise that it could take some time and may turn out quite expensive.'

'The cost is immaterial,' David snapped, 'can you do it.'

'Calm down Sir,' the gentle voice murmured. 'please call me Liz and yes, we can do it, but being such a long time ago, I doubt that the records will be on computer, so it will mean a physical search of dozens, if not hundreds of files. Now I need you to give me as much information as possible. Then you must write down everything that you can remember and post it to me as soon as possible. I shall need names, addresses, exact ages of the people concerned and definite dates and years. Have you got that?'

'Yes, yes,' David said quickly.

'In that case, please tell me about the person you wish to find.'

'Her name was Jennifer Allen. She shared a flat with another girl in Portsmouth at the time, but she told me that she came from Winchester. Her age would have been twenty or maybe twenty-one. I'll have to try and think back on that, but she worked as a secretary for an electrical company in Fratton Park.' David paused for breath.

'Is that all Mr Fox?'

David could imagine the woman at the end of the line waiting patiently for some startling revelation.

'I think I may have left her pregnant.' The dramatic words gushed out.

'You see Liz, I had known her for about two and a half years but it was a purely platonic relationship until the last night. When I left her, I promised that I would be back as soon as possible, but when I did eventually manage it, it was too late.'

'What do you mean, Mr Fox, too late.'

'Well, I went round to the house where she shared the flat, but her landlady told me that she had gone home to have a baby. Then as an afterthought she added and to get married. I'm afraid that at the time the only words that registered were, to get married. I'm afraid that it broke me up. You know, realising that I had lost her forever. I don't remember all the pubs that I hit that night, but I do remember being in the White Horse Inn on Southsea Common at one stage. It was a pub that we often used in the old days, though that night it was all just a blur.'

'It sounds as though it hit you quite hard Mr Fox. What happened next?'

'Well, driving back up country next day, I suddenly remembered the having a baby bit. I was so shaken that I almost drove off the road, so I pulled onto the grass verge to think about it. That was when it struck me that it may have been my baby. I mean Jenny didn't do that kind of thing lightly. I've lived with that idea for over forty years, and I spent a long time trying to find her, but without luck.'

The voice on the line became more businesslike. 'Right Mr Fox. I have all that straight in my mind. Now if you could write it all down and let me have it, I'll get onto it straight away. Thank you for calling Ajax.'

'OK I'll do it immediately and thank you.'

David drained his second glass of malt, reached over and carefully placed it on the small side table, then lay back in the chair and stretched his legs. His head still throbbed, seemingly in time with the dervish-like whirling of the crazy, mixed up thoughts.

'Two o'clock already,' he muttered, glancing at his wristwatch. 'is it really four and a half hours since David left?'

The telephone rang. Automatically he jumped to his feet, walked across to it, reached out and picked it up.

'David Fox.' he stated firmly. He heard only a faint click as the line went dead.

'Fools,' David snapped, as he tossed another generous dose of malt into his empty glass. 'Suppose I should think about getting something to eat,' he muttered, then took a heavy gulp of the spirit.

The phone buzzed insistently. David clamped it to his right ear.

'It's Liz,' the female voice said.

'Any news?' David murmured apprehensively.

''Fraid not. Not yet anyway. We've searched all the records for anyone named Jennifer Allen getting married in Winchester around the year you stipulated. No luck. So next we tried for a record of her birth, again no luck. So while we were there, we tried for a child born to a Miss Allen with the same result. It's almost as though she doesn't exist, unless it all happened somewhere else.'

'You know Liz, I had a feeling that it would be something like this.'

'Sorry, David. Do you want us to call it a day, or would you like us to try somewhere else. Perhaps Portsmouth. It could be that the landlady lied about her going home.'

'Yes, keep digging Liz, but keep me informed.'

'Will do. I'm already on my way. Bye.'

David slowly circled the room three times before coming to a halt at the window. As he gazed into the late afternoon darkness, he idly sipped at the malt. Suddenly, as though prompted by the spirit, another memory untangled itself from the jumble. He grinned as he remembered how he and Jenny used to sneak into the silent house and sit for hours on the cellar stairs just talking, after they had been to the cinema or perhaps one of the pubs on their list of suitable meeting places. Sometimes they would hear the landlady walk past the door. They would sit cowering in the dim light like two mice waiting for the cat to spot them, but she never did.

He remembered how protective the sharp tongued landlady was towards Jenny, although she made it perfectly obvious that she wasn't fond of him. David grinned again. 'She was a good hearted old battle-axe,' he told the open space beyond the window.

The ring of the phone chased the thoughts away. He picked up the hand set.

'Hello,' he said, 'David Fox.'

Again the click before the line went dead.

Some damn fool with nothing to do on Christmas Day, he mused, feeling a touch or irritation. He topped up his tumbler again and glanced at his watch. 'Four-thirty already,' he said loudly to the tree in the corner. 'Time flies when you're having fun.'

Standing before the window again, sipping at the Scotch and staring into the darkness of the early evening, he remembered that he still hadn't had anything to eat all day. Turning to the tree he said, 'Must get a sandwich in a few minutes.' Then he giggled and muttered, 'Do you know that you are the only friend I've got today. What do you think of that?'

He giggled again as he remembered that one dark January night Jenny had told him that she had received a pink, long handled back scrubber as a Christmas present. He had replied that someone was hinting that she shouldn't have anyone in the bathroom to scrub her back for her. For some reason they had both laughed at the time, although it wasn't that funny.

Another memory surged forward. They had been to the cinema. A film called *Hell Drivers* is remembered, staring Stanley Baker or some such name. Walking back to her flat later they had been passing a chemist's shop when she suddenly stopped and pointed for an advertisement for a new aftershave for men. It was called Corvette. Jenny had giggled and commented that corvettes were baby destroyers.

Another thought offered itself. Could she have been hinting that she was thinking of lovemaking that night. He mentally shrugged. If she had, it hadn't happened. It never did until that famous or infamous last night.

The phone rang again. David picked it up.

'Liz here David. No luck in Portsmouth I'm afraid. This is costing you a lot of money and going nowhere. Shall we call it a day this time? Are you sure that this girl really exists?'

'Oh yes, Liz. She exists. After forty years she is still my beautiful, blonde-haired angel. At least in my memory, but I think you're right. It's time to stop searching. Send me a statement and I'll let you have a cheque by return post. Goodbye Liz and thanks.'

'Goodbye David. Sorry we couldn't help you.'

He slowly replaced the handset and turned towards the window. He was momentarily startled by the sudden ring of the phone again. On the second ring he grabbed the noisy thing and snapped, 'Hello.' Again the line went dead.

'Damn it,' he shouted aloud. 'This is getting beyond a joke. He angrily slammed the phone onto its rest. The table rocked under the onslaught, but stayed upright.

Unthinking, David sloshed more of the malt into his tumbler and drank deeply, remembering how he had once tried to get Jenny to spend a weekend with him at Brighton. She had refused, so instead they had taken as ferry across to the Isle of Wight. He remembered that it had been a miserable, disaster of a day. That night he had picked a fight with her and finished off by storming angrily away, back to his ship. That prodded thoughts of all the other nights that he had angrily walked away and just left her standing on the pavement. At the time he couldn't even understand why he did it. He knew now. 'It was that bloody wall of friendship she had built around herself. It always left me frustrated,' he shouted out loud, waving his almost empty glass at the Christmas tree. His whirling thoughts reminded him that he had never been able to break through that invisible wall, and so he couldn't tell her how deeply he loved her. Not once in two and a half years had that love word been spoken and he was never sure whether she felt anything for him, but this silent love had controlled his life ever since. Tears for a wasted love rolled hotly down his cheeks. His throat ached with the tension inside him.

The phone rang again. 'If it's another damned hoax call, I'll leave it off the hook this time,' he slurred as he rolled unsteadily towards the table.
'David Fox,' he yelled into the mouthpiece.
'You sound angry, David. Problems?' A gentle voice asked.
Momentarily he felt stunned. His hands began to shake and his stomach churned.
'Jenny?' he eventually murmured, getting the butterflies under control. 'Is that you?'
'Yes, David. It's me.'
'Dear God,' he muttered, still feeling the effects of the sudden shock. 'Never in my wildest dreams did I ever expect to hear your voice again and you're lucky to get me. I was going to leave the phone off the hook. Some damn fool has been ringing me then hanging up without speaking. Where are you?' he added.
'At home and that was me phoning you, but when I heard your voice I couldn't speak,' she paused momentarily, then her words rushed out.

'David told me all about your meeting. He's delighted to have found his father at last. He says that you look well.'

'And I'm delighted at the way he's turned out. You and your husband certainly did a fine job of raising him.'

'But I never married, David. Didn't he tell you?'

'He wouldn't say a word about you, said he was under strict instruction not to.' David had to struggle to keep his words even as wild emotions raged inside him. Surprise, anger, joy, even sadness for her. All he could think of was, she never married. More unwanted thoughts. Why? She was beautiful then. Many men must have wanted her. What happened? He realised that he was speaking again. The thought had become words. 'Why didn't you marry, Jennifer?'

'Not now David,' she insisted. 'If I call you again then perhaps we can discuss things like that, but not now.'

'Will you give me your phone number?'

'No, David. I'm not ready yet. Remember, I'm not young anymore and at my age I don't need problems. Everything must be my decision and don't try to find me.'

'Funny you should say that. I've been toying with the idea all day. I even had mental conversations with a detective agency, but even they couldn't find you. Just out of curiosity, where do you live?'

'That doesn't matter. Promise not to try and find me.'

'I promise Jennifer, and you should remember that I always keep my word. Sometimes rather late, I'm afraid, but better late than never.'

'In that case, David, I'll tell you something that I should have said years ago, but I didn't want to damage your marriage at the time. I loved you passionately, David. Every minute from the moment we first met and even when you treated me badly, but I knew we could never be together.'

'But we can now.'

'Can we, David? Do you really think so?'

David thought he heard a trace of hope in her voice. He wasn't sure.

'Of course we can. I've never stopped loving you, even though I loved my late wife as well. I'll try to explain if you give me the chance.'

He thought he heard a faint sob down the line. Was she crying? Her voice was tremulous when she spoke again.

'I will call you, David. I don't know when, but I will. I need to think for a while. Goodbye, David.'

'Not goodbye. That's too final. Make it cheerio.'

'Alright, cheerio.'

Cheerio and always remember, I love you dearly.'

The phone line went dead.

THE ARTIST
Derrick Brain

The gates of Corsett Orphanage closed behind Norman Dobell with a clang. For sixteen years through a series of House Parents, Corsett's had fed, clothed and sheltered him. He had shared his toys, books and household chores between five other boys and six girls in 'his' House.

Quarrels were punished impartially, a lost meal, extra duties were hardships imposed as a matter of rule.

Once a baby stayed for several months, the girls learn how to wash, change and feed the mite, the boys thought it was fun until challenged.
'I dare you.'
Norman as the eldest was cornered under eight pairs of critical eyes. He prided himself on a job well done. He trembled, the babe smiled, the House Mother gave him a pat on the head.

The House Father taught everyone to mend a fuse, change a leaking tap washer or deal with a broken toy. Gardening was organised by the Senior Management - volunteers were given extra pocket money.

Sunday mornings he hated. Inmates were paraded in their Sunday best through the streets to the local parish church. The whispers and stares of the locals and visitors annoyed him.

Like many before him, six months before his sixteenth birthday he was called to the Principal's office and given the choice:
'You can have a flat and cater for yourself, rent paid, for two years. You can go into lodgings, full board paid for twelve months, or there is the hostel.'
Norman waited, hoping that Canada would be mentioned. The Principal's 'Well?' spoilt that dream.
'The flat, Sir,' he said with regret.

The House Mother fitted him out with the wardrobe of new clothes, checked the flat's inventory and helped him pack the few personal possessions he owned. A second visit to the Principal gave him a bank book, the Home's regular leaving gift, plus unspent gifts and earnings.
The rare difference in Norman's case merited the directive,
'I want to see you on your 21st birthday.'

As the echo of the clanging gate faded, Norman suffered a spasm of fear and loneliness. He was on his own.

His first employer had been arranged by Corsett Management. By his eighteenth birthday he had been with eight employers.
Fits of coughing he put down to smoking and he made a vow never to touch another cigarette. He never enjoyed his local inn - the smell put him off. Others might call him a miser but the pence he saved were added to his bank account.

For months a poster prominently displayed outside the coach station fascinated him. The painting of a lass, her long flowing hair, like her dress, tossed by the wind, framed in a setting of hills, cornfields and cottages. The caption underneath read 'A new life in Lodley Moor' and in smaller print 'twice daily coach service'.

Norman's reaction was controlled by a letter from the Principal telling him the rent for the flat would be so much.
Lodley Moor coach stop was part of a block of buildings, including a mini market cum Post Office, tobacconist and newsagent. At 6.30 on a Saturday morning, all that Norman saw was a taxi fast disappearing and a news vendor with a dozen different newspapers spread over a series of milk crates.
Leaving his luggage with the vendor, Norman strolled down the winding street. The fresh air tickled his nostrils. His sneeze became a cough but he dismissed his tiredness as part of night travel. A stabbing pain like a knife thrust into him and the next thing he knew was the soft sheets of a hospital bed.

To me, Norman was case number 178432 S B 243. The S B were my initials, Sheila Baily, the 243 my personal case number, while the longer figure was the departmental reference. He was three years my junior - an overgrown schoolboy with deep sunken cheeks and dreamy blue eyes. All I had to do was to fill in a few forms, get his signature and ensure that the Welfare State was working.

My second visit changed that. The moment I saw Peter Masterson seated on the edge of his bed, I simmered with jealousy, if not Cupid's dart.

For six months Peter and I had kept each other company. He was religious and I am not, so we drifted apart. As if Norman read our thoughts, his challenge rung merrily across the ward:

'Come on lass, get this zealot off my back.'

His eyes flashed, his cheeks blossomed and I felt a warmth inside me.

'Afraid Peter's not very practical,' I said, handing Norman a Sick Benefit cheque, 'I doubt if he can change that for you.'

'Oh yes I can.' Peter grinned, producing his wallet. 'And I know a couple who need some young life in their home. The Larkhams tell me they are coming to see our friend tonight.'

'Better unchurched than a couple of holy rollers.' I sniggered, annoyed that the news I carried was second-hand.

'If you two are going to fight,' Norman leaned back into his pillow, 'do it elsewhere. I want to see Miss . . . ' He stuttered, not knowing my name and adding, 'Alone.'

'Mr and Mrs Larkham are in their early fifties. He is the manager of our local store and she spends her time organising various charities - when Peter and I were courting we spent hours with them.'

The next time I saw Norman was at the Lodley Moor United Church Annual Gala, a day of festivities for all the family. The Pastor of Lodley Moor Mission, his colleagues from the Parish Church and the Methodist Minister tried to be on friendly terms, tactfully befriending lapsed members and in accordance with custom shared the profit.

Norman was propped up against Mr Larkham's stall of home-made wooden toys. 'Pops' as Norman called him from the first evening, made, sold or gave away dolls' houses, bread boards, egg cups, musical jewel boxes as a charity - hobby effort.

As soon as he spied me, he reached out and took my arm in his announcing, 'Come on lass, let's have a strawberry tea. Peter's just gone that way.'

I could have screamed. Peter was the last person I wanted to see.

My weeks of infatuation with Norman came to a sudden end. At twenty-six Arthur was every girl's dream, endowed with good looks and a charming manner. He was a member of the Aero Club and boasted of flying whenever he pleased.

His invitation to accompany him to the Aero Club's Annual Dinner sent a thrill through me and meant a hasty renewal of my wardrobe.

As Arthur and I became more affectionate, Norman, Peter and the Larkhams faded into the background.

When Arthur said he wanted to attend the Missionary Aviation Fellowship at the Methodist Church, it meant nothing to me. I remember little about that rally except that in the interval we came face to face with Peter. His greeting vibrated like an earthquake:

'How is the wife and babe?'

I stared at Peter in disbelief. He never winked or relaxed a muscle. I looked at Arthur without hearing what he said.

I dashed from the building, tears like a fountain pouring from my eyes. I left behind my coat and shawl, mentally unconscious of where I was going. I cursed Arthur for his deceit. I cursed Peter for his abruptness. I huddled by a lamp-post on Lodley River bridge. Life had become a living hell and it was as if the foaming waters called, 'Join us, join us.'

Was there a surge of prayer from that rally? Did Peter have behind his devastating words an anxious loving heart? At that time I did not care, as one step from a watery grave Norman saw me.

'Sheila, lass' he repeated again and again and within seconds I was held in his embrace. Firmly but gently he led me to Ma Larkham, where in garbled fashion I told them what had happened. Norman unwittingly added to my distress by jovially saying:

'You had better join my girlfriend in Canada. She had a baby for her fourteenth birthday.'

Pop's witty 'Yours, I suppose?' did not help.

I cannot say I dried my tears. I had lost Peter, Arthur's memory cursed me, Norman had a girlfriend in Canada. I groaned that I was on the shelf - a tainted wench.

In the weeks which followed, Norman treated me as he treated the girls at the orphanage. A little fuss, a little flattery, a teasing tongue and a listening ear. I did not know the pain that a visit to the orphanage caused him.

The Principal had come straight to the point.

'Your father was a soldier - a rifleman. You were six weeks old when your mother died. Your father, knowing that his father was on the Board of Governors, brought you here. Your father remarried and when he died he left behind a wife and your step-sister heavily pregnant. Your stepmother literally dumped her on our doorstep. Your father had earlier sent to us a letter addressed to you, to be handed to you on your 21st birthday.' As he spoke, he handed over the envelope, yellow with age and watched Norman impatiently open the missive.

'My Dear Son. I wronged your mother. Her parents found it hard to forgive me. Mr and Mrs Larkham were at the time missionaries in North East India. Grandpa Dobell and I quarrelled many times but he used his influence at Corsett.'

'Grandpa Dobell?' Norman queried, glancing across the desk at the Principal.

'He could not face your father's court martial and resigned from the Board of Governors - I believe he would like to hear from you. He is 82.'

Returning to Lodley Moor, Norman's silence was put down to extra work, an avalanche of mail. Some voiced the opinion 'If he does not slow down he will have another breakdown.'

It was during his days of depression that he came out of a block of offices as I went in. He invited me to join him in a cup of coffee.

Leaning across the coffee table, his eyes twinkled. His tongue wet his lips as we surveyed each other. I thought of the time when we had a strawberry tea, a memory marred by the day he held me in his arms on Lodley Bridge. I also thought of Ruth and imagined I was playing second fiddle.

'I have just signed a contract for the lease of a workshop at the craft centre,' he said, a trace of hesitancy in his voice, 'and I am scared.'

'Is Pop pleased?' It was a silly thing to say but I could not bring myself to say that I was pleased.

'He says I have stolen all his customers.'

'Have you?'

'He gave them to me and most of his tools.'

'Why?'

'They are returning to India on a short-term contract. Did you know that they are my grandparents - my mother's parents?

'No . . . ' I gasped and then stuttered 'Where are you going to live?'

'With you at the craft centre.'

'Oh.' My heart seemed to miss a beat as I asked, 'What about Ruth?'

'I am not allowed to marry my step-sister.'

'Oh,' I repeated as his hand reached across the table to touch mine.

'When my father died, my step-mother, knowing that I was at Corsett, literally dumped Ruth and her baby on the doorstep.'

'And you happened to arrive at Lodley Moor by chance.'

I grinned happily as his fingers gripped mine.

'Not quite. Great grandad is an artist. He painted the poster 'Lodley Moor in Springtime'. I never bothered to read the signature and when I saw him last week, he told me the lady was my great granny.'

'Now I suppose you will tell me that's Mr Dobell of Lodley Hall.'

'He tells me you arranged his home help and meals on wheels.'

BORN IN A FIELD
Jennifer Bailey

Didn't I ever tell you that story? Oh, it was years ago, a few months before Tim and I were married. He was still working abroad so I was house hunting. And not very successfully, either. Everything was either too small, too big, too expensive or too something else. Or else I was just too fussy. Tim had said he'd be happy anywhere.

Anyway, I needed a break so I escaped for a long weekend with my parents.

I was on my way back on the Monday afternoon. It was about two o'clock. I'd taken the A roads rather than the motorway and I wasn't far from Taunton when I passed a signpost to Stoke Bauchamp, 2½ miles. Now, as soon as I saw that name it rang a bell, but I just couldn't think why. I knew I'd never been there. It's not on the way to anywhere and it's not the sort of place you go to unless you've got a particular reason.

Then I remembered. Just before I'd left on the Thursday morning, the postman had delivered yet another leaflet from the estate agent. I'd had a quick look, stuffed it in my bag, meaning to have a proper look over the weekend, and then forgotten all about it.

Until now. The house, Teasel Bank, was in Stoke Beauchamp. That was where I'd heard the name. So I stopped in a lay-by and dug out the leaflet. It said 'By appointment only' but I thought I might as well take a chance and go and have a look. I could see the outside if nothing else.

Didn't take long to find it. Had the right name, too. It was set up on a bank covered with huge teasels. I rang the bell and after a few minutes an elderly man opened it. He was very tall, with a mop of white hair. But I'll tell you what really struck me about him - his eyes. Very blue, they were, with that clear, direct look of a child.

I apologised for turning up without an appointment but he didn't seem bothered.

'I've got to go out later,' he said, 'but there's plenty of time if you'd like to look round now,' and he introduced himself as Andrew Cotman.

I liked the house. I liked it as soon as I walked in the door. It felt, well, just right. As if I'd known it all my life. Comfortable. Familiar. It wrapped itself round me like an old coat. I just stood there soaking it up.

Then I realised Mr Cotman was saying something.

'Oh - sorry,' I said. 'I was just - well - feeling the house. It's so - so content.'

'It's always been like it,' he said.

'Have you lived here a long time?'

'All my life. My grandparents came here when it was first built, and my father was born here. So was I, but I'm the last of the line now. Emmy and me only had one son, Peter, and we lost him at Dunkirk. I've left everything to a distant cousin. He lives up north somewhere, so won't want this place. You won't have any trouble buying it. He'll keep it with the same estate agent.'

This didn't make much sense to me, but before I could say anything he'd gone into the room on the right.

And what a room! Uneven floor and walls, furniture that must have been there since the house was built, a very up-to-date television and central heating radiators. But yet nothing seemed out of place. 'Ancient and modern,' said Mr Cotman. 'We've always kept what we liked, whether it was in fashion or no, and added bits as we've needed them.'

'It's lovely,' I said. 'It's the sort of room that's grown over the years, not been created in a few days by a designer who'll never live here.'

'You'll add to it as well,' he said, assuming everything were already settled.

As we went out of the room, he closed the door behind him.

'One of my failings,' he said, 'leaving doors open. Drove Emmy mad. 'Born in a field, then?' she'd shout after me. Still fancy I hear her sometimes if I forget.'

He took me over the rest of the house, all the same comfortable mixture of ancient and modern.

'I may be old, but I'm not old fashioned,' he said. 'And Emmy and I never saw any virtue in washing under cold pump water out the back, just because our parents did, when we could have hot water on tap. One of the first places in the village to have a proper bathroom, this was. Funny how many people suddenly needed to 'spend a penny' as they were passing, even when they only lived just down the road. Loved to pull the chain, they did.' He chuckled at the memory.

When I'd seen inside, he took me out into the back garden. A small lawn, borders full of the old cottage garden flowers, neat rows of vegetables and, just outside the back door, a herb garden.

'Emmy's pride and joy' he called it. He said he'd tried to keep it going since she died a few years ago, but he hadn't got her touch.

But carrots - well, I was talking to the village expert. Carried off first prize every year since anyone cared to remember.

'Some people have even suggested disqualifying me,' he said, laughing, 'but they won't have to now. Someone else can have a chance, maybe that young Charlie Roper. He's been trying to beat me for the last forty years.'

I said I'd do my best with the herbs, although I'd never planted anything since I grew mustard and cress on blotting paper when I was five.

'You'll learn,' he said, 'My Emmy hadn't done any gardening either when we married. You're very like her, you know. I'll rest easy knowing you're here.'

We went back in the kitchen and he made a pot of tea and got out a packet of chocolate digestive biscuits.

'My favourites,' I said, 'You must have known I was coming.'

'Maybe I did, maybe I did,' he said.

While I drank my tea - he said he wasn't thirsty - he told me about the local amenities, the shop, the new hall, the school and his greatest joy,

St Peter's Church at the other end of the village. He was very proud to be a churchwarden there like his father and grandfather before him.

'Have you got any furniture?' he asked suddenly.

'Not much,' I said. 'A small bookcase, a coffee table and a couple of stools. I'm in a furnished flat at the moment.'

'You could buy the furniture here with the house,' he said. 'But don't be afraid to get rid of anything you don't need or like. I won't be offended.'

'But won't you want some of it?'

'Not where I'm going, my dear. It's only a small place.'

He looked at his watch.

'Well,' he said, 'I'll have to be off soon. Got to be at the church by three.' And he laughed.

'Another one of my failings, being late. Emmy used to say I'd be late for my own funeral. And I'd still like to prove her wrong.'

He looked like a mischievous little boy. I said I could drop him off at the church if that would help.

'Thanks,' he said. 'That'll save me rushing.'

I wandered around the garden while he got ready, then went back into the kitchen. Mr Cotman was rinsing my cup under the tap and didn't see me come in.

'Better leave it all tidy,' he said, apparently to himself. Then he just stood there with the cup in his hand.

'Yes,' he said, 'We've been happy here, haven't we, old girl. And they will be too, them and their boys . . . All right, I'm coming, don't worry. I'll be on time for once.'

He turned round to put the cup on the dresser.

'Oh, there you are,' he said. 'I'm ready to go now.'

He closed and locked the back door and made sure the kitchen door was shut as we went into the hall. 'Or you'll have Emmy after you,' I said.

'She'll be there,' he said.

Well, he didn't stop talking as we drove through the village, telling me who lived where and not just their life histories but their parents' and grandparents' as well. Eventually I managed to get a word in.

'Mr Cotman,' I said, 'I'd like to make an offer for Teasel Bank.'

'Do it through the estate agent,' he said. 'It's out of my hands now, but there won't be any problems. Now the church is just up that road on the right there. If you stop opposite the turning I can walk the rest. Only a hundred yards. For once I'm not late.'

I pulled in and looked towards the church. A hearse was just parking by the lych-gate.

'Well, goodbye, my dear,' he said, taking my hand in both of his. I noticed how cold they were. But cold hands, warm heart, they say.

'I know you'll be happy at Teasel Bank, as happy as me and Emmy have been.'

'You'll come and see us, won't you?'

'I'll do my best,' he said.

'I'll take that as a promise.'

He got out of the car, walked round in front and started to cross the road. I checked the rear mirror, then looked over towards the church to wave if he were looking. But I couldn't see him, not walking along the pavement or with the people taking the coffin out of the hearse. I reckoned he must have moved pretty quick for an old man.

Anyway, first thing next morning I was in the estate agents.

'Teasel Bank,' I said. 'I'd like to make an offer for it. It's just right.'

'Don't you want to have a look round first?' Mr Morgan asked me.

'I have,' I said. 'Yesterday. Mr Cotman showed me round.'

'Mr Cotman?'

'Yes, Mr Cotman, the owner.'

Mr Morgan picked up the local paper, last Friday's edition, found the page he was looking for and handed it to me, pointing to a paragraph in the Announcements column.

'Cotman,' I read. 'Andrew James of Teasel Bank. Stoke Beauchamp, peacefully at home on July 10th 1979. Funeral St Peter's Church, Stoke Beauchamp, Monday July 16th, 3 p.m.'

'He'd asked us to sell it,' said Mr Morgan, 'and I'd sent out the details before I knew he'd died. So it can't have been Mr Cotman showed round. Must have been a friend with a key.'

I didn't bother to argue. I just told him we'd buy the house if Mr Cotman's cousin wanted to sell it. And it all went through just as Mr Cotman had said, furniture and all.

He was right. We're very happy here, as happy as him and his Emmy. The herbs are doing well, and you've seen Tim's carrots for yourself.

We often take flowers, even carrot tops sometimes, and put on his grave. And when they were little, Andrew and James looked on him as an honorary grandfather. Even now they always go to the churchyard when they're home.

Does he come to see us? Oh, yes, he keeps his promise. We've never actually seen him but we know when he's around. Doors open apparently by themselves, even when there's not a breath of wind. No, it doesn't give us the creeps. We just shut the door again and shout 'Born in a field, then?'

TOM-THUMB CLOSE
Josephine Brogan

The close has some ornamental stonework where it adjoins the street and starts off under a high arch of dark-red bricks. But then it comes out into the open and runs on between two dykes, past some waste ground and allotments. It is paved underfoot all the way and the earth on either side is bright with nasturtiums that are trained over the dykes. At the path's end are two railway houses, two-storeyed and semi-detached, built almost on top of the railway lines. My grandfather and my aunt and her family live in one and an elderly couple with a seven-year-old daughter, a Shirley Temple look-alike, live in the other.

My aunt, though now in her fifties, has long hair, iron-grey, worn in pigtails for the work of the house or scraped back into a tight bun at the nape of her neck. Pretty mouth, clear skin and a delicate, straight nose. She is my father's sister, married to a whaler who walks with a rolling gait, feet planted wide to keep him steady. She frightens me to death - the few years I will spend with her will equate to half a lifetime. I know every bend in the dykes, every corner of the side-by-side gardens. I can draw up an inventory of the furniture. The girl who was her youngest child shines in my memory like a jewel.

She had inherited her mother's looks. Dark hair, eyes like nuts and smooth shapely legs. Patriotic too, joining the Women's Voluntary Brigade with her plain little red-haired friend and standing to attention during the Remembrance Day Service in her smart blue uniform and brogue shoes. Wild for the dancing like all the girls, over-riding the occasional maternal no-no and if not, going anyway, climbing through the small window of the room where I slept, shushing me, dropping her dancing shoes ahead of her by the side of the railway line and then off, picking her way lightly across the tracks, though the footbridge was only fifty yards away. Watching her on a Friday night, powdering and lipsticking at the small mirror that hung at the side of the sink and palming the seams of her stockings over her pointing toes, I wished with all my heart I could be grown-up too. Shirley Temple and I would rush to hang over the dyke as she passed down the paved path, her fuchsia scarf curling as she turned to wave. *Belle*. A Virgin Queen passing over the water amidst fireballs and fountains of colour, with the rattle of tambourines and smell of musk cleaving the evening air.

There were two upstairs rooms in the house with a door between opening directly on to a steep flight of wooden stairs. These led to an attic room with a skylight and two ancient box beds. This was where I mostly did my homework, lifting the skylight clear of cobwebs and dead flies to let in the air that smelled always of the sea. There I wrestled with Latin, did my trial-and-error maths, became intoxicated with the elephantine skittishness of Johnson and wept over trigonometry. Sometimes, in the middle of a hard Saturday afternoon, I would go down to the room below where the harmonium was. The sound-box wheezed and banged but I had my father's musical thumb and on fine days, I lifted the little sash window as far as it would go to let the sounds out. Drivers would wave from the trains that passed not twelve feet away and toot their horns. It was only towards the end of my stay, when I was nearly seventeen, that I discovered that in this room, some years before, Belle had given birth to a son.

* * * * *

Two of them came to see her, Belle's mother, stepping smartly in past the corner of the kitchen door and blocking the light from the window. One did the talking, the other interpreted and she saw the shoulder flashes on their uniforms clearly for the first time. The soldiers had arrived six years before, in the summer of 1940, taking up quarters at Arbroath and Carmyllie and Barry Links to the north and further south at Tentsmuir and Leuchars and St Andrews.

Now, hearing the measured, deliberate words, too loud for the small house, she felt intimidated. The officer's silver-grey hair grew thick and straight from his forehead and he held his baton as if it was a diploma. The heavy rumbling sentences succeeded each other without pause, punctuated by the flickering words of the translation, a mesmerising descant which allowed no space for any words of hers. They would take care of everything, all costs and there would be no scandal; she should understand that the man came from an old military family, of the best pedigree, but he was already married and there was no question that the child would be legitimised; there would be financial recompense should she require it. She gripped the edge of the kitchen table and waited till the words stopped. 'You have to go now,' she said and watched them as they turned to leave, laying her eyes along their straight Polish backs and feelings her legs shake.

That summer of 1940 close on 20,000 arrived in Scotland. In the dreadful chaos of the last days of June, after first Paris and then the whole of France fell to Nazi Germany, remnants of the Polish land forces struggled through to the escape ports of Bayonne and Bordeaux and La Pallice in Brittany. Officers and corporals, machine-gunners and engineers, sappers, orderlies and chaplains - almost all were brought to ports in Scotland. And by September, the brigades were assigned, concentrated in an enclave that took in the Counties of Angus and Perth and the Kingdom of Fife, that flank of country which curves round the agricultural riches of the Firth of Tay and is so vulnerable; and for the rest of the war the men of the First Polish Corps were stationed in the North. More than half were destined never to return to the regions of their birth. The calamity of his country sent the Captain wandering in many dangerous territories and at last he came to Scotland; only to find himself, like Aeneas, overwhelmed by love in a foreign land. All thoughts of the past and of the future blew away for the lovers in the warm winds of the cliff paths and in the evenings, she carried the touch of his arm home with her up the nasturtium pavement.

Now the mother said nothing to Belle. She was beset by anxiety but it was as if she had already decided - at once, as soon as she understood what the Major was saying. Her plan, born out of some old memory, was put in hand with scrupulous attention, her will-power straining against the ache in her heart.

And so - precious boiling beef, the finest that could be coaxed from the butcher, pale and glistening from the peppery soup, with particles of barley and onion lodged in its crevices. Thin slices of corned beef, stained with beetroot, laid out on the best plates. Rabbit from Young's on the Esplanade, cooked with rice. And always the harvest of the sea - juicy haddock, tiny curling dabs and skinned cod, used never as a dish for the family but only to make soup, simmered for an hour with celery and lemon substitute. Greeny-white cabbage from the allotment, judiciously spiced with malt vinegar and softened with tiny amounts of butter hoarded from the ration. And once a month on a Sunday, the large glass bowl brought down from the high shelf, for trifle sparingly decorated with imitation cream and larded with the tart raspberry jam that was made in small amounts every July. (I yearned for this to be repeated when I came to live but the bowl remained empty on the shelf, an enduring memory,)

Not any of this was done with Polish money. Some secret cache was broached in the days of her need and my grandfather ate with slow pleasure. Shirley Temple, learning to skip outside, chanted the rhymes *(I'm a girl guide, Dressed in blue, See all the actions I can do)* and made her complicated curls bounce. But the girl for whom the house laid out its finery sat without speaking.

* * * * *

'But what was it that happened. Leona, tell me, please,' I pleaded. I was in the drying-green, helping to fold the double union sheets so they could be hung straight on the line to dry. And at last she told me, leading me into the low wash-house and lighting a cigarette from the boiler fire. Belle's older sister, back living in the house after a broken marriage. Unconsciously she copied my aunt's movements, swiftly making two plaits of her hair as she held the cigarette in her mouth and screwing up her eyes against the smoke.

'The baby . . . What happened?'

'They were watching, watching for it. He must have been an important man but Ma wouldn't let them near her before. When her time came, Ma put the old man in the attic and the rest of us out of the house, snibbing the door. Took Belle upstairs to the room where the harmonium is and locked her in. Left her there to have the kid on her own, in the box-bed. Twelve hours and a big baby - she must have been out of her mind with fright . . . And Ma down in the kitchen through it all, smoking and smoking. Cleaning up the blood herself when it was over, before she went for the doctor. We didn't dare interfere. The locked doors. It was between Belle and Ma.'

'But, Leona, the baby . . .'

'We don't know what became of him. They came and took him as soon as the midwife finished. Some of the Poles had their wives here and there were the Scottish wives too. Ma couldn't stop them. The war was over and they were being demobilised. It was bedlam. We knew it was bad for them because the Soviets were in control in Poland and half of them refused to go back. But I suppose *he* had no choice really - his wife and children were in the western part, outside the new Soviet frontier. Then a couple of years later, all the borders were closed. So they never saw one another again.'

'And now . . .?'

'It's all behind them now. Ma loves Belle the best.'

I knew that. The look in the mother's eye told it all. The waiting up till she got back from the dancing and the hot-water bottle in the bed. The blue uniform pressed for parades and new nylons every week.

'Did she ever hear, you know, from Poland . . .? Any sign, any news?'

'No, not ever from him. But the officer, he sent her perfume. Dear stuff, a big bottle all done up in a fancy box. Foreign.' I smelled the musk, sweet, with sharpness behind.

That Friday night she was off again, down the close and along the street, catching the bus for the city. A stunning girl, with a wide smile.

She was being courted by a butcher and presently would marry him. I didn't care for him - bad skin and his teeth too big. My aunt didn't care much for him either. But her daughter was *article endommagé,* damaged goods.

What I minded most was that she would never have crocodile shoes or eat Beef Wellington or sleep in a Paris hotel. I still mind that. Such beauties arrive only once or maybe twice in a lifetime and should be cherished. I mind it too that the Tom-Thumbs no longer tumble over the dykes nor do the sheets fly in the breeze, for, all these years later, it's as if my grandfather and the soldiers and Shirley Temple never existed.

A COUNTRY PAS DE DEUX
Maryse Durand

In the house everyone was asleep except Denise who was wide awake. Married for twenty years, she had given all of herself to her husband; children, a well kept house, tasty cooking.

All seemed perfect, but in their busy routine the lack of real companionship with her husband affected her deeply.

She was fifty years old and lived in a safe cocoon, with no financial problems, and had lots of friends. She had given all she could, and yet loneliness possessed her.

Who was she? Was she fully happy? She tried to go back to sleep. Tomorrow will be another day.

At sunrise she got up; and had a quick breakfast.

She did not know what made her go a different way with her small car. She drove for miles, far from the city.

Taking a deep breath, she saw she was in a strange country lane, when her car engine started smoking. She stopped and opened the bonnet; then gave a big sigh. It seemed hopeless, smoking like that! She looked to the left and to the right, but all seemed deserted. Then she saw in the distance a little red-roofed cottage between the trees.

Without hesitation she made for it. The small gate said: Château Cézanne.

She knocked at the old oak door. When it opened, a handsome, shirt-less man appeared. 'Yes,' he said, 'How can I help you?' She explained about her car breakdown and her predicament.

He said, 'Come in, but please don't look at the mess - I'm used to it!' Canvases hung on the white walls, and more were stacked against them. Tubes of paint and bottles with brushes littered a big table.

'Did you paint all of these pictures?' she asked.

'Yes, of course; but let me introduce myself. My name is Gilles, a bachelor and a broken-down artist.'

She looked at him while he spoke. God, how attractive he was! It was summer and he hadn't bothered to dress beyond his blue jeans trousers and shoes. His torso was lean and muscular and his sunburned skin looked silky. He noticed her look and said: 'Excuse me, I must go and put on a shirt; then we'll both go and find out what's happened to your car.'

He went to another room to get dressed, while she looked around, admiring his work. What talent! she thought. They are very good!

Five minutes later, he came back and said: 'That's it, I'm ready. Let's go.'

The car was parked a mile or so away and seemed to have been just dumped by the hedge. He examined it for a while then said with a serious expression, 'I'm very sorry, but the engine is quite dead!'

'Oh, my God!' she said, her hand to her mouth. 'What am I going to do?'

'Let's go back and I'll telephone a garage.'

They returned to the cottage and he started ringing up. After three urgent calls, he said, 'I'm sorry but it's impossible to get anyone before tomorrow.'

'Oh!' she exclaimed, bewildered. 'then where can I spend the night? Is there an hotel anywhere near here?'

'No,' said Gilles, 'but I have a double bed here, if you can put up with such poor accommodation. I'll sleep in the hammock.'

She asked if she could ring home, to tell them of her car breakdown.

He left her alone with the telephone but overheard some sentences. 'No! I can't possibly come home tonight. Look after the children, I'll be back tomorrow. Yes! I found a place where to spend the night. I kiss you. See you tomorrow.'

He watched her from a distance. She was so good looking, so elegant. Yet there was a certain sadness in her eyes. She was married with children.

She hung up and thanked him, and he asked her if she'd like a drink.

He brought cups of coffee and they sat at an old table.

Their nearness and sharing brought about a change in both of them.

She lowered her eyes and seemed troubled. He broke the silence by asking her about her life. Somehow she felt she could tell him anything; all her life without embarrassment, without restraint. It was the first time she had ever confided in anyone that way. Then in her turn, she questioned him. He had been separated for a long time. His only passion now was painting, reading and classical music. They talked non-stop for an hour or so, until night caught up with them.

Suddenly he said 'Good God! My loneliness has gone, talking about myself like that to you; but I haven't offered you something to eat! Come into my kitchen. We'll cook something.

They sat side by side, she had helped him to cook a satisfying pasta with tomato sauce.

It was as if they had always known each other. They drank some wine, and then an embarrassed silence followed, as each waited for the other. Finally and almost shyly, she asked: 'May I go and see where my bed is?'

He showed her the bedroom with the big country bed. Then it all happened. He took her in his arms and she did not resist. Desire was there very quickly, as much for him as for her. An amazing physical attraction.

They undressed and made passionate love, as if to prove perfection to each other. She had never, never felt such a powerful attraction before. The whole night through they held and slept together; knowing love and loving-kindness.

At first light around six o'clock, they were both awake and filled with intense love-emotion, laced with great sadness. She had to go away and they had to part.

At eight the doorbell rang. It was the garage mechanic.

Two hours later, the car was ready to go. She looked into Gilles' eyes and said, 'Adieu. It was wonderful!'

He kissed her and whispered, 'You will come back, we know this cannot be farewell. Now you will have to choose.'

Was what she had found by chance, the answer to her loneliness? Passion, love, a soul mate, true companionship, the meeting of minds, as well as bodies, that is so complete and overwhelming, that it can seem stronger than any security and safe routine? Tomorrow might tell. Perhaps only God knew.

THE HAUNTING
Betty M Burton

I first saw the little ring at a local Antiques Fair held in a church hall in Ilkeston.

It was only a plain gold ring, but I was drawn to like a magnet and bought it without a second thought.

Not usually given to 'impulse' buying - it was quite out of character for me, but in this instance I seemed quite powerless to resist it.

There were some initials engraved within its circle - almost worn away but still just visible. They were DHL.

That momentary lapse from the usual was to be my first step into events of an even more unusual nature.

It was several weeks later when the first shock came. It was a dismally cold afternoon and the rain dripped miserably down the classroom windows where I sat marking Arithmetic books whilst thirty heads were bent over desks, and minds more intent on the portents of last night's video nasty were struggling with précis. I heard the classroom door open and close, and soft steps coming over to my side. I didn't look up for I guessed it was young Mr Yates or 'Yocker' as he was known to the staff and children alike.

He would be wanting the list of names of the lads wishing to go on the Adventure Holiday he was arranging. I had foolishly agreed to go alone and act as general 'nurse,' being the only member of staff to have any medical knowledge, and of course - the fact that I was the daughter of a doctor. Old Gregson the Biology master was 'too old now for such capers.' The fact that my 'medical' knowledge was purely veterinary seemed of little consequence and any way we all had our St John's certificates.

There was a discreet cough at my elbow. 'Ay up, watch out, Harris has just passed a lewd drawing to Clegg.' I looked up quickly. Cyril Yates the Geography master was idly perusing some papers on a clipboard. 'Ah' he smiled, catching my eye on him. 'I wonder if you would be so kind as to let me have the list of Adventure Holiday boys Freda?' he asked in his usual polite way. Absent-mindedly I handed him the list. 'There you are, only six going I'm afraid - family cash shortages, I suppose.' He took the list and left the room.

Had I been dreaming or had I really heard that remark about Harris and his drawing? It hadn't sounded in the least like Cyril Yates. Indeed it wasn't his kind of phraseology.

Curiousity unleashed, I stepped with cat like quietness over to Clegg's desk, just in time to see him stuff a piece of crumpled paper under his exercise book and continue writing, looking the picture of innocence. I was taking a risk, I knew, but I had to prove to myself that I had not imagined those words about a 'lewd drawing.' Swiftly, and before the startled Clegg knew what was happening - I pounced on the exercise book.

There was a crude, but wickedly recognisable cartoon of Miss Flamstead, more coarsely known by the boys as 'Passion Killer Ivy' - due to the unfortunate fact that a particularly windy day had revealed to a homebound group of them that Miss Ivy Flamstead wore silk 'bloomers' under her sensible tweed skirt. The cartoon showed a somewhat bony Ivy in full flight from an astounded looking Mr Dorelli - the language master, who had a 'balloon' coming from his mouth encircling the words 'Por Favoré and in his hands were a pair of bloomers. My hand itched - and I smartly clipped Billy Harris on the back of his head. A gasp went round the class and Harris blurted out 'Ar'l git me Dad ter yo. Ay'l gi yer wot for!' Before he could add any more I almost spat at him: 'You do that, and your Dad can come and collect this . . . article from the Head, whilst you apologise to Miss Flamstead. Of course' I added, 'The Head, Miss Flamstead, Mr Dorelli, and myself can always pay a visit to your Dad with your work of art!' I safely knew that Billy's Dad - 'Boxer' as he was known - would hand out the thrashing of Billy's life - if so confronted; but I also knew that I had to get 'my spoke in' first or 'Boxer' would be just as likely to march down to school, and 'set about' me for 'assaulting' his precious son.

Luckily Bill Harris withdrew from the mounting aggression and muttered something that passed for an apology, but was much more likely to be an oath of future harassment.

I walked back to my desk and sat down heavily. I found myself twisting the ring about on the fourth finger of my right hand. I was breathing rapidly and my heart was pounding, but I distinctly heard the voice in my ear quietly hiss 'You should have hit the little bugger a bit harder while you were about it!'

I looked round swiftly but I was alone with the thirty desultory scholars - and the classroom windows were Lachrimose with the fine drizzling rain and found an echo somewhere within my heart. The voice had an educated air about it, but even so, was strongly tinged with a local accent.

I had been teaching at Heanor, Eastwood and Ilkeston now for sixteen years, and to my sharp South Glamorgan ears (I hailed from Cardiff), I could pick out quite a few local accents around Nottinghamshire and Derbyshire. How did I come to hear the voice? Apparently no one else had.

There was a clatter of desk lids and thumping of books and a general hubbub of voices in heated discussion, and glancing at my watch was startled to find it 3.25 p.m. already. Those little horrors may be illiterate, enumerate, and generally indisposed to learn, but each and everyone seemed to possess an unfailing, in-built time clock within them. Admittedly it went somewhat 'on the blink' on their journey into school, but was always in a good state of repair for their outward journeys. 'Right, hand in your books as you leave, and don't run down the corridor and *make less noise!*' I yelled after their rapidly retreating bodies. The last one out seemed to trip over something. 'Ow!' howled an outraged Kevin Clegg as the falling Harris grabbed him before both fell in a heap on the floor. Billy Harris's expletive was quite unrepeatable.

A soft laugh came in my ear and I distinctly heard the words, 'Little sods! They don't improve any.' I jumped up, and looked wildly around me. The classroom was empty. Everything was the same as ever, including the musty smell of books, chalk, dust, unwashed bodies and ancient heating pipes.

I shivered. It had gone perceptibly colder. Picking up my well worn briefcase - I fished my purse out of the desk and left the room.

A few evenings later on returning home from a rather long service at our local church I made myself a cup of hot chocolate and sat down at my treasured old piano.

It had belonged to my father, who had spent what few free hours he had in his busy practice to unwind at the keyboard. He had been quite a talented pianist who had, in his youth, yearned to play the concert grand on board one of the great liners as resident pianist.

Leafing through some old music scores, I picked out one or two of father's old pieces. Blumenlied, Vilia, Marigold, Clair de Lune, and Widor's Tocata.

Glancing at the score of the last piece I promptly put it back. Definitely beyond my talents. Playing for a school concert was decidedly less taxing than attempting the requirements of Widor's striking musical extravaganza.

I now ran my less talented fingers gently over the keys and started to play one of his favourite tunes. The room was dark except for a pool of light shed from the old table lamp on my left. The air felt chilly in spite of the fire glowing in the grate.

I rubbed my hands to ease the stiffness of my fingers, and noticed that one of my fingers had swollen. I tried to remove the little gold ring to ease the finger, but the swelling held it fast. Again I began to play. The piece was Claude De Bussy's 'Clair de Lune,' and its gentle notes suited my mood.

It was when I was just about to turn over the first page that I heard it. A faint sound almost like a sob or sigh, and it came from the direction of the little footstool to my right - near the piano.

Poetic words were softly spoken in a cultured voice - but ever so lightly tinged with a local Eastwood accent. It was the same voice I had heard in the classroom. I knew now, and all at once, I knew something else too. It seemed to happen when my fingers made contact with the little ring I had purchased from that Ilkeston Fayre. The words I had just heard spoken were familiar ones, the last few lines, from a much loved poem, but I couldn't for the life of me, remember who had written them.

I was annoyed with myself. A teacher of English literature and I couldn't even remember the local author of a favourite poem 'Piano.' 'Freda,' I said aloud, 'You're growing old!' 'Oh no,' another voice contradicted very softly. 'Frieda will never grow old.' It continued, 'Play again, mother, play again, *please* . . .'

A shiver ran down my spine for the voice had now subtly changed into that of a small child, and grown fainter. Something brushed lightly against my leg and as I put my hand down to investigate - I felt the touch of icy little fingers on mine. The coldness shot right through me and even as I jumped and pulled my hand away I saw something glittering roll away under the piano.

I looked at my finger. The swelling had gone, and the ring had slipped off.

In a frenzy I rushed to put the room lights on and then, kneeling on the floor I scrabbled around for the missing ring, but in vain, and I couldn't move the heavy piano to retrieve it.

I could have sworn as I felt along the edge of the piano a voice almost sighed into my ear - 'It was mine and I'd given it to my mother. I kept it to remind me . . .' it trailed away, and there was silence in the room. A silence that almost - breathed - but the air was warm again and somehow I knew that my 'haunting' was over.

From that day in 1965 to this day, the ring has never been found.

A Brown Owl
A Bhambra

Brown Owl came especially to collect my friend and I to take us to Brownies. It was our tenth session and I had learned a lot, how to thread a needle and how to sew buttons. Dad was pleased with me when I sewed back his shirt button. Christy and I were best of friends, we always went out together. Every Saturday morning we would visit our local cinema.

The Brownies were holding a special celebration in which all the pack from all over Britain were going to attend. Christy and I were very excited about the party. I polished my badge as usual. I went through mum's clothes and found her brown slip with brown lace at the bottom. I liked it, so I decided to wear it under my uniform without mum's permission. It was too long so I fold it at the top. We went to call for Brown Owl who lived only a few doors away. She had a lovely grandfather's clock in the hallway. It was so quiet in her house, and the only thing you could hear was the tick tock of the clock. She was in her 50's and always wore the Brown Owl uniform. Her hair was always neat and tidy and she always had a smile on her face. She was so kind. She picked up her cardigan and we followed her out of the house. We walked back to the school to greet the other members of the Brownies.

We all got on the coach and after half an hour, we arrived in a woody place, where there were other coaches from other parts of Britain. It was a very special day for all the Brownies. There were well over 200 Brownies; we played games together in groups. While we were playing, a couple of Brown Owls came up to me and took me inside the building. They were smiling and giggling and two of them helped me with my mum's slip, which was almost down to my ankles. Then they took me and another English girl to a room which had a huge cake, to cut it, while the photographers took pictures of us all. I was so shy that I just about managed to smile.

We had a lovely day out. During the end of the week my dad spotted my picture in the local paper. He was really proud of me, as I was the only girl chosen out of 200. Could it be because they pulled me out of the crowd because of my mum's sexy lacy slip?

RUINS ARE US
Robert D Shooter

She watched in anguish as her husband, her young husband as she saw him, lurch unsteadily as if drunk, from church gate to seat. Yet it was only ten in the morning and she knew for certain he had not had a drop. He didn't drink. Well, not that he was teetotal. He just drank at special meals, or a pint of cider on a ramble or cycle ride. Or a malt whisky drunk slowly beside the open fire.

Normally he would have been lost in thought in seeing a new church. His poetry-scribbling book would have been out noting down insights caught by the stone, the atmosphere, the dedications, or simply the spirit of the place, which hit him. Only now, most unusually, she was walking round the ruins, praying in the bit with the roof still on, praying madly that he was not having a stroke. That at fifty-seven he still had vigour and life for some years to come. That the first holiday without any of their four kids was not also the last.

Yet he was still looking dazed. Not in wonder at the seventh century Saint Barr's holy ground and its relics, or its more modern graves, including some poverty ones of today in this beautiful Hebrides Island, but it was as if he himself was hit. Hit with something, which was debilitating him. Something which was at the moment tearing through his body; something with which he was only just being able to retain reason, consciousness and speech. She noticed without really noticing the flowers to a loved one buried in poverty. They were not far from a more elaborate one to a famous writer who adopted himself to these islands and had a cottage within spitting distance of his grave. Yet today her husband was not noticing these things. Today he was absorbed in wonder at his own frailty. And she was deliberately keeping her distance. Not because she did not love him in sickness and in health; but because there was nothing that she could do. It was loving to give him space to find himself. If he couldn't she would be with him in no time.

She moved on behind a wall still standing. It was partly to see what was behind. It was also so that should he be looking for her, or at her, he would not see her tears. That would ruin it for them both.

When she reappeared the other side of the wall he had disappeared. She could see him nowhere. How could he disappear in such a place? Well easily I suppose, she thought, as she just had. Maybe he was crying somewhere. She noticed him come out of the bit with the roof on, he was blowing his nose as well as holding the back of his head. The part, which he had said, vibrated, throbbed with pain. But he was standing. He was looking outwards towards the top of the wall into which she had disappeared. She made to wave but he walked towards the wall and he was almost straight. In fact his meandering could have been deliberate to take in the more interesting bit of ruin as he passed. If so that would be the more he.

She moved back to make as if looking at the poverty grave she had just left and he joined her in a few moments.

'Poverty burials in this beautiful spot,' she said to him, pointing.

'Yes,' he said. 'I noticed. Beautiful it is. Not a bad place to die.'

She looked at him. 'Or to live?'

He looked at her. 'Lovely place to live.'

Her heart missed a beat with the hope, which throbbed through in that reply. 'Dare I ask if you feel a bit better?'

'The dizziness, the being unbalanced as if out of control has passed. The throbbing pain remains but is not quite so bad so often. What do you think it is?'

'I don't know.'

'I thought it was a stroke,' he admitted. 'At fifty-seven that would have been tough. Just when we've a bit of time together.' He smiled at her but then winced. 'I think it must be a muscle spasm or something which is really nasty but not serious. I hope so anyway.'

'Better go and find a doctor?'

'Yes,' he said, 'Or, if they have one on this island a physiotherapist.'

'Can you cycle to Castlebay or shall I phone for a taxi?'

'Let's try cycling there as originally planned,' he said, kissing his wife. He added, for some reason unknown to him, 'thanks.'

She kissed him back with such passion that he suddenly knew why. 'You had me so worried,' she said.

'Me too.'

They kissed again as an even older couple looked round the grounds, smiling at the passion of youth as they saw it, and a younger couple, possibly on their honeymoon, looked on in hope.

BEYOND THE TOMB
Duchess Newman

The searing heat rose in dancing waves upon the dunes. Egypt was not a place to be taken lightly. Weary tourists trolled about the desert, gazing at the endless amount of ancient relics, but for archaeologist Sally Harper this was an every day event, and a full time ambition.

Deep down in the depths of yet another opened tomb, it was her job to oversee that the retrieved artefacts were carefully wrapped and crated properly.

Some of the finds were so rare and fragile that it had been decided that she would personally crate them herself, here in the tomb, before they were brought back up into the living world.

A small table and chair had been brought down for her to work on, and a scary mass of wires had been rigged up to provide light, and a fan. Even so, the sheer weight of this great tomb seemed to have its own kind of claustrophobic atmosphere, and even with the fan going at full pelt, it still felt uncomfortably stuffy.

Sitting on the floor, his head in sleep, was a small Arab boy, who had persistently managed to attach himself to her.

At first she had considered him a nuisance, but soon came to depend on him when she needed something from one of the other workers up above.

It was much too hot to constantly clamber in and out of the tomb, so she sent Ali who was more than happy to go.

All he asked in return was something to eat and a little money. This was the way Ali had lived all his life, like so many other children here in the desert.

She glanced at her watch and noted just how long she had been underground. She had to get some fresh air and laboriously worked her way to the huge stone entrance.

As she emerged into the open she covered her eyes, but the brilliant sunshine seemed to pierce the cover of her hands.

There was great activity in every direction. Large groups of workers digging, and not seeming to mind the heat. Most of the locals worked for low wages and never tired during each days heavy schedule.

She stood there a while taking in this productive scene, they were on schedule. Entrance passages to every tomb, for some yet unexplained reason were only three feet high, and this made getting to the main chamber a real labour of love.

She laboriously made her way back, each step down the grooved causeway taken with great care.

Many an archaeologist had broken an ankle or leg by being in too much of a hurry. She sat back down at her table and resumed her cataloguing. Then the silence broke with the shuffle of feet coming down the passage.

She looked up and saw Martin Dempsey her field manager. She had met him in a bar in Malibu, and as he wanted work, and as she needed a young man to run her diggers so they teamed up.

He was ex marine and had been bumming about for a couple of years, but was now out of money. He was used to handling men, and fitted the bill.

Sally gave him a free hand and everything on site seemed to be going well.

He gave her his daily report on how the digs were going, and she was well pleased. An offer of dinner too was on the agenda, but Sally wanted to stay and finish up the tray she had been working on.

He had got used to her rebuffs. Her career was definitely her main priority.
He bid her goodnight and left. Sally beckoned to Ali and he shook his small frame and rose. She gave him a little money to buy some food and he was gone along the passage at full speed. He did not have to bend almost in half, and she could hear his cheap sandals scuffling along, and then silence.

Working all day in the tomb did not worry Sally, but she had noticed that as soon as she was alone an eerie feeling came across her, she had felt it once or twice before.

She gazed down at the table and her eyes fell upon a beautiful necklace. It was gold and decorated with jet and lapis lazuli. She held it to her neck with closed eyes and just for a moment tried to imagine what it must have been like in ancient Egypt.

She did not realise it but she had thought out loud, and had spoken her thoughts. All at once the chamber filled with a light breeze, a perfume she did not recognise. She opened her eyes and the papers on her table were gently lifting.

Then she got the strangest sensation, and the hairs on the back of her neck stood up. She raised her eyes and to her utter amazement, right in front of her stood a young Egyptian woman.

Dressed in robes that she had only seen on tomb wall paintings. She gulped and sat staring at this beautiful stranger.

Then to her utter shock the woman spoke. You enter my place of eternal sleep, and take away the treasures for my after life. Why do you do this?

Sally was to say the least gob smacked! She tried to answer, but could not utter a single word. She could feel her knees knocking and told herself that she had been working too hard and this was some kind of hallucination.

She promptly shut her eyes, and for a moment just sat there, trying to put her tired thoughts together, then very slowly she looked up.

The gold threads in the folds of the woman's dress shimmered in the reflection of the light. Her eyes were outlined with the deepest blue black dye and her whole body was adorned with breath-taking jewellery.

The woman stared at Sally and was equally taken aback by her khaki shorts and chukka boots. The sight of a pretty woman dressed like a boy confused her. Sally gathered up all her nerve and asked her who she was. The woman smiled and told her she was a princess, and her name was Neffala.

Sally returned the courtesy by telling the woman her name also. Then an uneasy kind of silence fell on them both, neither knowing just what to say.

You wonder about my world in old Egypt, said Neffala. I can take you on a journey there if you wish to go. It is within my power.

Sally really did think she was going crazy now, but the thought of living such an adventure was too hard to resist.

'What would I have to do?' she blurted out. 'Just take my hand' said Neffala 'and close your eyes, and leave the rest to me.'

Sally did not feel very easy with any of this, but was so curious that she rose and stepped forward reaching out her hand.

Neffala took hold of her hand with a strong grip, and immediately Sally felt a weird sensation she could not describe.

A strong sense of dizziness came over her, but it only lasted for a few seconds, then as she opened her eyes, her breath was taken away with the sight that lay before her.

There she stood in the hustle and bustle of ancient Egypt.

She had been transported back five millennia, and she did not know how she had got there. The whole scene was a riot of noise and colour, and she did not know where to look first.

'Come' said Neffala, 'we will go to the palace where I live.' Sally did not answer, but followed her like a puppy dog, frightened of losing sight of its mother.

There were strange odours and many costumes she had never seen before, and her poor frazzled brain was desperately trying to catalogue everything, but so much was going on that it was an impossible task.

Straight in front of them was a huge columned building. The entrance had a massive parade of steps. Sally followed behind this beautiful stranger, and as she reached the top of the steps turned to survey this wondrous scene before her.

They passed through many large opened rooms, till they came to one all draped in white linen.

The servants standing either side opened the curtains and they entered. This is my room of sleep, said Neffala, as she gestured to the couch.

It was rather like the couches the ancient Romans used. Everything in this was very beautiful. Fine perfume bottles, casks of jewellery, lavishly patterned cushions of every colour.

Neffala walked out onto the balcony and beckoned to Sally. The view took in the whole square below and the lesser streets beyond.

It was early evening and two female attendants entered the chamber and lit the large oil lamps. They silently went about their duties, eyes cast down, not even noticing Sally.

Neffala told Sally that soon they would join her other family and guests for feasting. She clapped her hands and two hand maidens appeared. She pointed to Sally and gave them an order. They hurried away and returned with armfuls of beautiful robes for Sally to try on.

Sally's head was still spinning, but she dispatched with her T-shirt and trousers and proceeded to put on each robe with sheer delight.

She was spoilt for choice. There were deepest shades of blue, and the richest weaves of warmest peach. All were interwoven with threads of gold.

She finally chose a pale turquoise blue, with a gold braided belt. Neffala took a large gold pin from her dressing table and placed it on her left shoulder.

We must give you an Egyptian name, or someone might think you are a spy. I will call you Cira.

Sally was again surprised. I did not know you had spies in such early times. I only thought it applied to my era.

Men without scruples have always been ready to do anything for a bag of gold. Neffala helped her comb her hair and line her eyes, then she put some perfume on her neck.

You will come with me now, but will walk one step behind me, do you understand? Sally nodded. I will tell them you are my old friend.

As they approached the doorway, the curtains opened as if by magic, but it was only the two servants who had to stand there all day.

The massive size of each room was just amazing, all had lofty pillars and floors of marble.

The sound of talking and laughing became clearer as they got closer to the feasting hall. Her heart began to pound, she was sure they would hear it.

Then Sally could see them, a large group of young men and women laying on couches eating and drinking. At the head of the room was an elderly man wearing a head-dress that denoted he was the Pharaoh.

He caught sight of Neffala and beckoned her over. Come sit with me, I haven't seen you all day. What have you been up to my daughter.

Neffala gestured to Sally and explained that she had been meeting her friend. They sat down and food was served to them, Sally was thrilled but equally terrified as they ate their meal. The opulence of this gathering was totally stunning.

She had never seen so much gold in her life. It adorned everything, and the array of precious stones was breathtaking.

Sally did more looking than eating. It was hard to try and take it all in. Then all of a sudden, a strange thought leapt into her head. How as she going to get back to her time and reality. Being here like this and watching the life that she had only seen in tombs and drawings was a dream come true, but she had no wish to spend the rest of her life here.

She turned to ask Neffala about this, when the sound of a huge gong echoed around the room and a troupe of dancing girls entered. Then there were acrobats and finally some wrestlers.

The feasting and entertainment went on long into the night, and as Sally had been up since seven o'clock in the morning, she was feeling totally worn out.

Finally it all came to an end and Neffala rose, bowed before her father and began to leave.

Sally shuffled behind her trying to look inconspicuous. Her mind racing.

The gentle breeze gently wafted through the long open hallways. Sally looked at her watch, in her time it was three thirty.

In their absence, the servants had brought another couch into Neffalas room and Sally just about managed to whisper a goodnight, before falling full clothed onto it.

It was extremely hot when she woke and she looked around for her host, but she was alone. She passed the time trying on all the beautiful jewellery that lay on the marble dressing table.

There were many thoughts running through her head, she had always imagined that a place like old Egypt would be totally disorganised, but her impression now was just the opposite. Everything was so well thought out and there were a strict set of rules to obey, laid down by the Pharaoh.

The wisp like curtains opened, and Neffala entered the room. Dressed in a flimsy white robe, her hair decorated with plaits of gold, she was truly elegant in her way. Sally had made up her mind to ask her lots of questions, to get as much information as she could.

Neffala seemed to pre-empt her thoughts and started to relay all kinds of things about life in this vast oasis in the desert. Nomads had first lived here since time began all coming from many different places, so Egypt was like a huge melting pot.

They sat on the veranda and talked for hours. Sally wished she had her laptop. All of this was too good to forget.

It was late afternoon, it was something you sensed. There were various ways of telling the time here, like sundials and water clocks, but these were stationed outside.

Two attendants entered with fruit and wine. As they refreshed themselves Sally asked Neffala the question that had been on her mind. How do I get back to my own time?

I was granted this gift of after life travel, by my Gods, I can take you back when you want to go.

Why did you enter my time Neffala? You awakened me, was the reply . . .

The usual feasting went on late into the night, and no one questioned her being there. The next day they travelled to the outskirts of the city and Sally's eyes nearly popped out of her head. For there right before her eyes were thousands of slaves, toiling away in the gruelling heat, and yes! They were building the great pyramid.

She froze in amazement. This great effigy was yet unfinished. Everywhere she looked both men and women were performing some back breaking task.

Sally explained to Neffala that the pyramid was classed as one of the wonders of the world in her time.

It was just a tomb for the Pharaoh, was her reply. Each important ruler must have his or her house of rest. It is the stepping stone from this world to the next, where we will live amongst the stars.

Sally sat down on a boulder, her eyes took it all in but her brain was having a great battle. It was like a computer refusing a wrong command.

Neffala told her they had to leave now as she had promised to visit a sick friend. With great reluctance Sally rose and they made their way back to the city, and she felt quite sorry for the attendants who had to carry their sedans.

The shade of the walled alleyways gave some respite from the heat, and finally they stopped at an old wooden gate.

They entered into a beautiful courtyard dressed with masses of lush green plants to give much needed shade. A tiny pool sparkled in the sunlight.

They were ushered inside and there lying on a couch near the window was a lovely young woman. She was thin and pale, and Sally could see at a glance that she hadn't left this house for a very long time.

Her eyes lit up as Neffala walked towards her. She sat on the edge of the couch and spoke to her.

Sally edged forward and spoke a few words. The girl replied with a faint smile.

The mother of the house brought refreshments and then readily sipped the fruit juice. Then Neffala rose and caressed the girl with great tenderness, and they departed.

You are wondering who she is. At one time she was my personal attendant and true friend.

Then one day she was taken ill and she is just getting weaker by the day. The Priests and holy men have no idea what ails her, they have tried everything.

Back at the palace they relaxed and took refreshment, and Sally tried to explain some of the wonders of modern medicine. Neffala listened with great interest, but Sally got the impression that she did not believe her.

In Neffala's spirit like state she only had the confines of her tomb to transcend, so she would have no idea how far the world had advanced.

Sally had no idea how long she had been here in old Egypt, but as each day went by, she had expected, and Sally explained that it was much more than she had ever thought it would be.

They agreed that Sally should attend one last feast, so they rose and dressed themselves in the most beautiful of gowns, and adorned their hair with flowers.

As they sat in the huge feasting hall, Sally struggled to take in every tiny facet of this beautiful place.

The time rushed by and all at once it was over, and everyone was making their way back to their quarters.

Back in Neffala's room, Sally suddenly felt quite tearful. 'Don't cry' said Neffala, 'you will remember me sometimes.

Now are you ready to return to your own time and era?' Sally reluctantly nodded. 'Then take my hand and close your eyes as before.' With one last look around the room, Sally closed her eyes and the strange dizzy sensation again took hold of her.

Sally stirred, and opened her eyes. Her head was resting on her hands. She quickly sat up. She was in the tomb. She looked all around, but Neffala was nowhere to be seen.

A slight breeze wafted through the tomb and Sally was positive that she could smell Nefala's perfume, but she was quite alone.

Then all her thoughts began to rush round in her head. Did she dream it all. She was sure she had not.

She fumbled in her pockets, trying to find anything that could prove her magical journey, but there was nothing. She picked up her handbag and pulled out the old mirror that she carried with her. One glance showed her that there was no black eye make-up, or any other signs of her adventure.

She put on her jacket and made her way down the passage. When she finally walked out of the tomb, it was night. The sky was deep velvet blue and bejewelled by a host of glittering stars.

She got into her jeep and drove back to her hotel. There were still people floating in and out, and no one thought it odd that she should come in so late.

She laid on her bed and all the vents of her time travel spun about and her thoughts were so vivid that she could not sleep.

As she made her way back to the tomb in the morning, she entered with a caution she had never felt before.

She worked hard all day, looking up now and again, half expecting to see the lovely Neffala, but to no avail.

She decided to finish work early today and even told Dempsey that she would go for a drink with him, much to his amazement.

They sat in the corner of the bar, and Dempsey could tell that Sally had something on her mind.

'Tell me,' he said. Sally smiled uneasily and explained that he might think she was a crazy female. He joked that he had known many females like that. She beckoned for him to get them another drink, then blurted out the whole story.

Dempsey shrugged his shoulders, and shook his head. 'It's a real doozy' he said, 'the best I've ever heard.'

They talked about this unexplained event all the way back to the hotel. Dempsey did not believe a word of it, but humoured her because he really liked her.

Work on the tomb continued without any unusual happenings, then one afternoon Ali came running into the tomb and in his scrambled English conveyed to Sally that they had found a new set of steps.

She followed him back out into the strong sunlight, Dempsey was on his way towards her. He ushered her to the new find. It was indeed a new set of steps leading down to yet another unopened tomb.

Work progressed on these steps for over a week, till a flat stone doorway had been uncovered. The seal was unbroken to the great relief.

But there was something different about this seal. It was written in a form of picture writing that none of them had ever seen before. Dempsey looked at Sally and sighed.

They realised that this tomb was much earlier than any of the other recorded ones in this valley.

Then something strange happened, a light breeze wafted past them and Sally stepped forward and began to read the script. Dempsey looked at her in amazement. How did you do that? I don't know said Sally, I just did.

After days of sand shifting and planning, they finally opened the doors. Bent double as usual they made their way to the main chamber, there in the centre was a huge sarcophagus, and the whole of the coffin and all the walls were covered in the strange writings like the seal.

Sally started to read the texts, and Dempsey just stood there taken aback, because no one had ever seen this kind of script before.

Work took another two years to complete and in that time Sally had catalogued all the tomb writings. On her return to the States she published her findings, but work on the scripts was not taken seriously.

All through her working life she uncovered many great finds, always with Dempsey at her side. She republished her findings many years later, but still the writings weren't given any serious recognition.

Dempsey had found the girl of his dreams and was now married with two kids, but he always went with Sally on any new digs.

She had travelled the world and written a few books, becoming quite famous, but the writings of the Princess Leyla tomb had always grated on her mind. She knew somehow that her translations were correct, although she did not know how she had read the ancient, unknown text.

She had a feeling deep inside that Neffala had helped her, but she could not tell all the other archaeologists her secret thoughts. They would think she was crazy.

She retired and bought a house on the beach, where she took great pleasure in walking her dog.

Each month she had the archaeologists gazette delivered to keep up with all the news and events, which she read with great relish.

She browsed through it and her eyes fell on one article in particular. Over in Syria a script specialist had been working on some old pieces of stone and found a rare kind of script he had never seen before. After eighteen months of work, and many nights without sleep he had managed to unravel the secrets of this ancient picture writing. But the icing on the cake was that it matched the writings from the Princess Leyla tomb that she and Dempsey had worked on many years before.

This proved that the catalogued work from so long ago was accurate. A large smile spread across her face. This was the kind of news that people like her dreamed of. She lounged back in her armchair, reliving it all. Her time with Neffala, she knew now was true, and she had travelled back to the old Egypt and had seen that writing whilst she was there.

No one would ever believe her of course, except perhaps Dempsey. The peace of her day was soon to be shattered. She had not been the only one to realise the spooky way she had read the tomb script so long ago.

It was a reporter who wanted to write an article, and offered a tidy cash sum to print her story. It was he who had suggested to his readers, just as a page puller, that only someone who had seen the ancient script, in a previous life would know the origin of its meaning.

Little did he know how true his absurd statement really was. She agreed, why not she thought. Retired archaeologists don't make too much money to live on. The article was duly printed and television interviews followed, all with ridiculous amounts of money on offer.

At seventy-two years old she had become a celebrity. She was asked many times how she had managed to read the tomb script fifty years before it was translated, but she would just smile and say, the spirits of the dead live on in those tombs, perhaps one came back to help me.

No one believed her, but she was asked to repeat the story of Princess Leyla's tomb many times and ended up living her remaining years in luxury and comfort.

Dempsey was there, when she was finally laid to rest, and just for a split second he thought he smelt an unusual Egyptian perfume floating on the breeze.

Sally rests with the angels, but her story lives on and is repeated to all would-be men and women who follow in her footsteps.

Our world does not just belong to those who live in it at the present, the souls and spirits of the departed too have access. Perhaps there is a level where both can meet and just for a short time blend one with the other.

Remember, life is a circle, no beginning, no end.

A FAMILY TALE
Lorraine Ereira

I do think I'm a lucky boy. I have a wonderful family, and I know they love me very much, but sometimes I can't help feeling a little different.

I suppose it's because Mum and Dad treat me differently from my two brothers. I am the oldest and although this brings certain privileges, I still feel a bit left out sometimes. I do look very different from my family. This in itself sets me apart. I don't have the same abilities as my two younger brothers, they are able to do so much that I can't do.

However, I'm very close to my brothers. I love them both for their different qualities. Jack has a great sense of fun and an absolutely inexhaustible supply of energy. I loved to play with him. David on the other hand is gentle and kind and has always showed me such affection. We did a lot of things together, like playing in the garden and in the road we live in with all the other children, family days out and visiting relatives, but I always felt like the one who was adopted.

I arrived in my parents lives before my brothers came along. I don't know whether they thought they couldn't have children or not but I'm only just over a year older than Jack, my middle brother, so it wasn't long before the three of us became four and then a year and a half later there were five of us.

Things felt different when Jack was born. I wasn't the centre of attention any more although they were always careful to include me. However, it wasn't long before they would leave me behind sometimes when they all went out and then when David arrived it only seemed to happen more. You probably think that it is terrible that they went out without me when I was still so young, but they would never leave me without making sure I was well looked after and if they were going to be away overnight I always went to stay with really lovely people who would spoil me rotten, and then my family would always make a huge fuss of me when they returned. I would always miss them so much and sometimes I felt sad that they didn't take me too. I guess deep down I knew it was because I was different and not because they didn't love me. I would wait, counting every minute until they returned and when they did they would always make it worth waiting for. My brothers and

I would roll around on the floor together, roughhousing. Dad would always join in too, whilst Mum went into the kitchen to rustle up something good for tea.

Occasionally we went to visit my real mum and sister and my half brothers and sisters. They lived on a big farm, about half an hour's drive from our house. My brothers loved to go and visit and I would feel proud to be the focus of all their attentions. My real mother was always very welcoming to us all and although it was always fun to see them I knew my real mum could never have looked after me the way my adopted parents do. My real father didn't live with her and she always looked so tired. I suppose she just couldn't manage all of us on her own.

I even knew my real dad. For a while I saw him quite a bit but he was usually short-tempered and I knew he didn't really want to know me, so eventually Mum and Dad stopped taking me to see him.

After my real mum died we never went back to visit the farm and I lost touch with my sister and my half brothers and sisters although as far as I know they all still live there.

Like I said I did have privileges that my brothers didn't get. I was always allowed to stay up the latest, and when my brothers were in bed Dad and I would usually go for a walk together. Sometimes he would chat away to me - he always seemed to be able to share his worries with me. I would always listen intently to his problems or to the tales that he wanted to tell me. Other times we would walk in companionable silence. Dad and I had a special bond. I looked to him for guidance and trusted him like no one else. When we got home I would sit in the middle of Mum and Dad and watch TV with them. This was my special time, and I guess I loved this the most. I never really had many of my own friends, but always got on very well with my brothers' friends. When they came to call for them, they always invited me to go along too, and we would spend long, summer days building camps in the woods, or playing football on the green.

Early one summer when Jack was little more than a baby, he fell and broke his leg. Mum had not long had baby David and both of them needed her attentions more than ever. Although I was only young myself, it nearly broke my heart to see such a tiny little chap suffer like that. The only comfort I was able to give was to sit or lie next to him and let him know I was there. I desperately wanted him to jump up and play with me, but somehow I knew he couldn't for a while. Mum and Dad always said I was a very good boy during that time, but all I felt was the need to be with Jack. It had been difficult for all of us, but by the end of the summer I had my playmate back, his energy more boundless than ever.

I remember when Jack and David both got guinea pigs. I really wasn't too keen on small, furry animals and at first although I was curious about them, I really didn't get involved when they went to play with them. It made me feel left out as I watched them all together, but Jack and David desperately wanted me to befriend them and for their sakes I felt my curiosity and indifference change to a genuine feeling of friendship for these small, simple creatures.

We've all grown up a bit now and my brothers have started to go out more and more. I know they still really love me, but they do things that don't include me so much now. They've both got girlfriends and although I do like girls, I've never had more than a very quick fling. My parents never encouraged me to have a girlfriend, but I don't really mind. I'm quite happy to be at home, but if I hear them come in I always get up to see them. I love to hear about all the things they've been doing.

Don't think that I mind being different because I really don't. I love my family and I wouldn't change anything at all, given the choice. I think that I have a very special place in my family and I have never felt unloved or uncared for. It is my place to be here for them and to protect them as best as I can. It's just that every once in a while I find myself wishing I was a real boy instead of a dog.

THE EPISODE
Moira Thorburn

She abhorred the colour yellow and for some unexplainable reason the paper added an extra cruelty to the letter. Letter was rather an overstatement as it was really nothing more than a cursory dismissal note. She had glanced at the ending first and knew that it was bad news. Hard to believe that things had been so different only a few weeks earlier. Slowly she read the offending article.

Amanda
I do not wish for you to visit me here. I have a girlfriend arriving shortly and she will be staying indefinitely. We plan to get married next summer. I tried to tell you during my visit but it either did not come across or you did not listen. I'm sorry I did not mean to hurt you.

Goodbye, Bruce

After reading it over and over again, Amanda's body shook and shivered for what seemed like an eternity and sleep was something she thought she'd never experience again. How could life have gone so wrong? For 29 years Amanda had been in total control and now she felt like a crystal glass that had shattered on the floor. Her mind wandered to the last year when Bruce had been on the other side of the world. His job had something to do with his government and Amanda had never delved too deeply into that always accepting that he was unable to say much. When they had finally met up again 10 weeks earlier they had not seen each other for 9 months. There had been telephone calls and letters. Little messages to keep the emotions alive. Yet it had not been without some nervous doubt that Amanda made her way in a taxi at 5.00am that July, Saturday morning to the airport. Heathrow Terminal 3. What if her feelings had changed? If his feelings towards her had also altered.

She had promised to be there on time and was glad to be early. Waiting slightly behind the barrier she saw him come through looking to see if she was there. As soon as Amanda spotted him she felt like a character out of some cheap, romantic novel and not the independent woman she normally was. There were no words to express her happiness to its full. She likened herself to a jigsaw missing the middle piece and was now complete. Nobody before had managed to be more than an edge piece in her life.

They greeted each other with their usual 'Hi mate, how's it going?' They wrapped their arms around each other and it was as though they had never been apart. Splitting his luggage they made their way by taxi to the hotel.

The room typically expensive for airport hotels seemed rather spartan. Amanda noticed there was no chair. They caught up on bits and pieces of the latest news and after a cup of poor quality powdered coffee they drifted together in a relaxed state on the bed. Had they really not seen each other for so long. As they kissed Bruce gave out reasons for them not being together. All Amanda could feebly utter was 'I know.'

Not once did he mention what would turn out to be the most important reason of all. Someone else. Amanda had spent many years killing off every female emotion in her body but with him it was different. She had known it would be like this from the first time she had seen him. Her whole personality had changed since meeting Bruce. Now she was quietly confident instead of feeling the need to take on the whole world and beat it into submission. Funny really, when one would never have considered him to be her type.

They slowly began to explore each other's bodies. Amanda found it almost impossible to believe she could feel this good or want and need more and more of the same. As they were enjoying each other Bruce uttered the inane comment that they shouldn't be doing this as Amanda was too nice. They lay together for hours tenderly kissing, hugging tighter and tighter, wrapping themselves around each other with fingers, hands, arms and legs entwined. Nothing was rushed and Amanda felt totally where she belonged. Her place in the universe. It Nirvana existed she had found it. Making love was wonderful and they both lay happy and content.

Later they ventured out for a meal and Amanda introduced Bruce to the idiosyncrasies of British Rail and the Underground. Never was there a space between them as they walked or sat with their arms around each other or hand in hand. They spoke about everything and nothing.

Back at the hotel they made love again and Amanda silently wished she had the courage to be more adventurous. They slept in a glowy warmth with Bruce's arms cradling her and their bodies lying like two spoons in a cutlery drawer.

The next two days seem nothing more than a blur to her now as they spent most of the time driving around the country, catching up with friends, neither had seen for a while. Amanda remembers conversation being slightly strained on occasions on the return journey to London. Bruce mentioned something about being between chapters and going through a period of reorganisation in his life and he kept asking her what the matter was. Amanda was glad that the sun was shining and she was wearing dark glasses as she was beginning to become a bit sad at the prospect of their forthcoming unavoidable parting. Music was playing and Bruce had complimented her 'Clever as well as beautiful'. The former of these stimuli had always been guaranteed to influence her emotions and the latter although she had in the beginning always answered back with a smart, cocky comment, lately she had let herself believe they were genuine.

Back at the hotel they were given the same room as on their previous visit and somehow that lent an extra romantic feel to the air. Everything appeared settled again. At their evening meal Amanda had rather too much to drink and Bruce began to get depressed about his forthcoming assignment. He longed to return to his roots. Whenever anything bothered Amanda the first thing she lost was always her appetite and she sat at the table picking at her food. She could only focus on random bits of the conversation and by the time they went upstairs she was desperately trying to remain calm and in control.

Amanda was first in bed and when Bruce joined her he put his arm around her, kissed her and said 'Goodnight'.

The tears she had managed to hold off until then began to flow. His touch was so important to her that was all it took.
Bruce said, 'You've got to stop this.'
Amanda replied with a quiet, 'I'm alright.'
Bruce added, 'No, you're not.'
Amanda, 'I'll be OK.'

They began to make love and although Bruce was his usual tender, caring, gentle self, Amanda felt like a charity case as though he was making love to her not so much because he wanted to but because he thought it was what she wanted and that he somehow owed it to her in some perverse way. For the first time they had problems and although Bruce seemed to have an endless amount of patience all the time giving encouragement and taking the blame for the problem, Amanda sensed something strange and immediately clammed up into her Cancerian crab-like shell. They managed to give each other some comfort but Bruce uttered that it might be better if Amanda forgot about him. When pushed, however, he could give no reason for this apart from the fact they had a long separation in front of them. To Amanda this was of no importance as they had already survived one long parting and she knew that her feelings were strong enough to live through another. She tended to be rather like an ostrich and stick her head in the sand. When they were apart what she didn't know about couldn't hurt her. Ignorance on these occasions was bliss. The rest of the night was long and both of them were exceptionally restless and thrashed about a lot.

They hardly spoke after his early morning call. Bruce was obviously not looking forward to his journey. Travelling in virtual silence to Heathrow and there as he checked in Amanda summoned up all her courage and said., 'The underground is over there and as you seem unable to talk to me I might as well leave.'
Bruce's reaction was to hand out an address. For some reason which Amanda will never understand and she will regret as long as she lives, her next action will always be uppermost in her mind. She stepped forward, wished him all the best and after kissing him about-turned and without looking back left him in the airport and went to the underground. Unknown to Bruce the tears were streaming down her face and unknown to Amanda she had just said her last words to Bruce. As the train pulled out of the station she wanted to go back but she knew she mustn't.

Now all that is left is a pretty box of momentoes, tapes and letters. The smell of him has long gone from his old T-shirt. Words from a song on one of his tapes, a Richard Marx number, has a particular importance for Amanda now as there is now this emotional gulf between them as well as the physical 4000 miles.

'Wherever you go, whatever you do I will be right here waiting for you. Whatever it takes or how my heart breaks I will be right here waiting for you'.

Looking back Amanda can console herself with the fact that some people never find happiness as they journey through life. Although Bruce was only physically present in her life for 70 days for the other 385 although not by her side he influenced her every thought, feeling and desire. Even now he will continue to do so for a long time. Considerably longer than the episode.

THE PORTRAIT
Norah Buck

Young Laura skipped on excitedly, ahead of her mum, long dark plaits bouncing to and fro. It was her turn at spending two weeks of summer term at Nana's. So proud was she, wearing her pretty waffle dress, her three sisters at home having the same, only different colours. 'I chose the lemon one for you, as it compliments your hair. Brings out the auburn lights.' To satisfy her daughter's inquisitive, young mind, the definition of 'compliment' was explained. 'Forever asking questions,' Mary would often tell herself 'Still . . . she's a brain . . . learning all the time I suppose.'

Laura came to an abrupt halt, allowing her mum to catch up with her. Her hand clasped within Mary's, this warm July afternoon, her thoughts settled on her Nana. This fifteen minutes walk allowing her time to visualise this house. This house which continued to hold such great fascination for her. Mum and Dad's home contained only two rooms, not forgetting the scullery. Scullery the substitute for 'kitchen' during the early fifties. Well, especially within the northern working class, that was. Her Nana's house . . . well, so spacious it was, consisting of three floors . . . even an attic. In possession of a most vivid imagination, there remained an awareness of mystery within this house she so loved. 'Dear Nana', she thought. Oh how she adored her. Her lovely, large blue eyes mirrored a great sadness at times, failing to pass unnoticed by this observant child. Laura's mum, blessed with the same blue eyes, resembled her Nana, except her hair was chestnut brown and her lower jaw didn't protrude. There were no scars, no deformity. Mary interrupted her thoughts. 'Now be good for your Nana,' knowing full well Laura didn't need reminding. Well . . . not really, but just the same.

'The door's unlocked, Mary,' Anna Brown called out, on hearing the knock at the scullery door, 'just lift the latch.'
'Mm, you're making me feel hungry, Mam.'
'If you've time to stay awhile, I'll cut you a slice, once it's cooled down,' her mum suggested, on taking the large cake out of the oven, immediately testing it with a fork.
'I won't have time, Mam. Have to prepare Bill's tea. He has an early finish on a Friday.' Anna nodded with understanding. Her eyes settled

on Laura, noting the look of longing expressed in her deep blue eyes, as she gazed fixedly at the delicious smelling cake.

'Yes, you will be having some cake with your tea.'

Anna had answered her grandaughter's silent question, while smiling down at her with genuine affection.

'Ouch,' cried Anna, as her hand slightly brushed the hot oven, while shoving in the plate pies.

'Does it hurt much, Nana?' asked Laura, concern evident in her voice, as she swiftly went to her beloved Nana's aid.

'No, not much . . . soon be right as rain. Nothing for you to worry about,' she assured her grandaughter, while placing her hand under the cold water tap.

'Looking forward to your fortnight's stay, pet?'

'Well, bye Laura,' said Mary, after kissing her mum farewell. 'See you in a fortnight.'

'Bye, our Mary . . . pity you haven't time for a cuppa,' interrupted Emma, busily polishing the sideboard, 'expect you're wanting the usual meander round the rooms, eh? Remember Laura . . . not the small one.'

'She knows,' assured Anna, outstretched arm beckoning her. Laura snuggled up close to the comfort of the middle-aged woman's breasts. A small hand sought the wonderful silkiness of the long, black braid, which reached her waist.

'Laura? would you do a message . . . for my black bullets. Oh and my packet of snuff. Keep the change for sweeties.'

'Thank you Nana,' answered Laura, giving a nod. On her way out Laura encountered Jean Hepworth.

'Hello Laura,' she acknowledged, while pegging out her washing in the adjoining backyard. 'Tell your Nan, I'll call in tonight,' gave a nod continuing, 'I'll suggest another sing-song around the piano Saturday . . . tomorrow night.' Laura loved these events. Uncle John would play the latest tunes on Nana's piano, everyone singing along with such gusto.

'Laura,' spoke Uncle John, during tea, would you go to the newsagents for my Topper and Beezer?' She loved how he'd quietly chuckle while reading them. He'd passed them onto her this time. 'There pet, as promised.' She felt quite grown-up at that moment. Oh, how she idolised John, being so tall and handsome, with his sandy hair and blue eyes so like Nana's.

'He's so clever,' she'd often say, 'training to be a draughtsman.' There was also Aunt Emma, having developed polio as a child. One foot turned noticeably inwards, resulting in a pronounced limp. She remained adamant this wouldn't deter her love of life. Laura held great admiration for Emma, being able to help her Nana with the housework. 'And Emma must be happy', she'd convince herself 'she must be . . . she sings a lot'. She did indeed, and so sweetly.

Laura knew of her older uncle . . . Matthew. She'd never encountered him, but understood to be in the small bedroom, first landing. She'd observed her Nana passing to and fro with a bowl of water etc. Assumed him as being bedridden, Anna having to attend to his needs.

'Nana,' spoke Laura at well past her bedtime the following night. 'Could I listen to Radio Luxembourg . . . just half an hour?'
'It's late, I'd expect you to be really sleepy after our shindig tonight.'
'What's that mean?'
Here we go again thought Anna, before explaining the meaning of 'shindig'.
'By the way . . . I saw you devour the cheese.'
'Wha . . .?' Anna quickly interrupted.
'You know what devour means, told you not to, so near bedtime.' Anna nodded knowingly at her grandaughter, while pulling her down on her lap.
'Don't want you having nightmares,' Laura came in swiftly hoping to change the subject.
'So can I listen to Radio Luxembourg?' Anna sighed.
'Suppose, but not too long . . . expect you'll want to read in bed?'

Twenty minutes passed. 'Nana?'
'Ye . . .s,' spoke Anna apprehensively.
'Can I brush out your hair?'
'You're pushing your luck, little lady.'
After seemingly careful consideration Anna relented and smiled.
'Well . . . suppose . . . I'll enjoy being pampered.'
Laura began brushing out her beloved Nana's hair. 'Dear Nana' she thought sadly. 'had such a hard life in the olden days'. She'd absorbed snippets of conversation not intended for her young ears, concerning Anna, from Jean and Tom next door. 'Still does . . . having Matthew

who can't walk to look after . . . and her being old'. Still slowly brushing out her beloved Nana's hair, her subconscious mind drifted to her face.

'Nana, how's your face like that?'

'Er . . . er . . . I fell off a swing when small. My jaw was injured very badly . . . had to have an operation.'

'Does it still hurt you Nana . . . the scar?'

'No, Laura, it no longer hurts.'

Laura, a wise child, and overly sensitive to people's feelings, felt this was untrue.

'I'm so glad it hurts no more,' and left it at that.

That night in her bedroom, top floor of the house, she looked out of the window. She gazed, mesmerised at the wonderful view of the twinkling stars, so brilliant against the dark night sky. Tonight though, nothing could erase from her mind the story of the incident in the park. After what seemed an eternity, she finally went to bed. Reading only a brief time, her eyes drifted to the portrait hanging just to the side of the bed. A large portrait presented a very handsome little boy, dressed in an old fashioned blue suit, his large brown eyes revealing a hint of mischief. This portrait constantly intrigued her. Those smiling brown eyes seeming to draw her like magnet.

'It's late child,' scolded Anna, on entering Laura's bedroom. 'Time for shut-eye,' at the same time handing her a small chocolate bar. 'Typical of Nana' she thought fondly.

'Nana, who's the little boy in the portrait?'

'The little boy is Uncle Matthew . . . he was four,' she answered about to leave the bedroom.

'What's wrong with him?'

Anna stiffened, 'Er . . . he was taking shelter from the rain. Was thirteen at the time.'

'Questions,' thought Anna in despair, 'so many questions.'

'Then a tram suddenly collided with a car, swerved, mounting the pavement, Your uncle was almost killed.'

'Is there something wrong with his legs?'

It was difficult giving Laura answers to these questions. After all, she was only nine, though undoubtedly had an old head on young shoulders at times.

'Well, what is wrong with Uncle Matthew? Must be something . . . being in bed all the time.'

'It's his mind, Laura . . . just his mind . . . nothing wrong with his legs.' Anna's eyes became bright with unshed tears.

'Now don't you fret. Leave any worrying to me. I take good care of your Uncle Matthew.'

This Laura already knew.

She finished her chocolate bar, then gave one long, final look at the portrait. Her eyes lingered on Matthew's. Was it her imagination, or did his smiling, brown eyes really transform into great sadness? Was he trying to tell her something? With hesitation she switched off the bedside light, Nana and Matthew in the forefront of her mind. After much tossing and turning, sleep overcame her. 'I must have had a bad dream' she thought, awaking to discover her cheeks wet with tears. She lay still awhile, the dream so vivid in her mind. She'd pictured a youth, about thirteen, having black hair and large brown eyes. Same eyes as the small boy in the portrait. Only these eyes held such intense fear, his mouth opening, trying to speak, but no sound escaped his throat. He appeared as transfixed, glued to the spot. Just a few feet before him, his eyes focused steadfastly on a beautiful lady, struggling desperately in freeing herself from the brutish grip of some strange man. Laura could see this lady's eyes, so full of terror and despair. Eyes so familiar to her. Could be her mum. But no, impossible. She wore an old fashioned dress. Could be Nana? No, couldn't be. This lady was young . . . and her lower jaw didn't protrude. Then Laura saw something which glistened against her white throat. A knife. Laura recollected this being the precise moment she'd awoke. She gave a deep sigh. 'it was only a dream . . . a very bad dream.'

With a sudden rush of adrenaline, Anna began, with trembling hands, gathering together the used crockery. 'Do try and eat,' she said, concerned eyes on Laura's lowered head. The butter dish clattered onto the hard floor, shattering into pieces.

'It's OK, I'll see to it,' Anna insisted on hearing the scraping of the chair. Anna's hands, shaking, began to collect together the fragments.

'Ouch,' she cried out.

'Nana' Laura yelled out, forgetting in that brief moment her horrific experience of the night before.

'Does it hurt?'

'No, child,' she answered, swiftly covering a bleeding finger with a handkerchief retrieved from her dress pocket. 'It'll soon heal,' adding affirmatively while quickly heading for the scullery. 'Eat your porridge.'

A bloody finger under the cold, running tap, in silence she wept, consciously ignoring the throbbing pain profoundly eminent from her wound. To Anna, this was nothing compared to her mental anguish, this torture. Here, with a vengeance, were the events of that fateful night emerging to the forefront of her mind. Back to haunt her. For so very long she'd presented an air of normality. Shrouded herself in an invisible cloak. Her tear-filled eyes settled on Laura, clearly visible through the small opening of the doorway. Laura sat, motionless. Sad, questioning eyes beneath a deeply furrowed brow, gazed unseeingly towards the scullery. Porridge untouched.

To say Anna wasn't deeply concerned for her beloved grandchild, would be an understatement. A sigh rising from deep within, she softly murmured, 'Physical scars heal, given time, but mental? That's different.' She finally commenced the dressing of her wound. 'Must do my best to convince the bairn it never occurred . . . wasn't real . . . was a nightmare. Shouldn't have eaten the cheese . . . simple as that.'

THE ANGEL OF BERMONDSEY
Jonathan Dwelley

Six o'clock in the evening. Standing on the pier I did not know what to think. She had appeared on a barge, some fifty metres down river, as if from the mists shrouding the Thames. At first she paid no attention to my presence, her eyes followed a cruise boat gliding towards us. Then she turned and looked at me. A beautiful face - distant, it showed no expression, until she smiled. Why was this young woman standing on a rusting barge off Bermondsey embankment? And how did she get there?

'Are you alright?' I called out. She just smiled back, a gust of wind blew long black hair across her face. She once again cast her gaze at the cruise boat that was now passing the pier. The boat seemed to interest her deeply. She had begun calling out at me. I heard nothing. The chugging boat drowned her voice. She stopped, regained her composure and once again I saw her shouting silent words.

'I can't hear you, do you need help?' she shrugged her shoulders and smiled again - an innocent playful smile that quite confused me. Then she was gone. I was stunned. My eyes scanned the empty barge creaking at its mooring. She must have jumped; every week people end their lives by jumping into the Thames. I ran like a madman down the pier straining to see any sign of life in the murky water and swirling currents, nothing but driftwood bobbed on the surface. I pulled out my mobile and frantically called the emergency services. My heart pounded like thunder, 'Come on answer!' A pause, 'Bermondsey pier. Yes near the Angel! Quick! I can't see her.' While waiting for the police, I paced along the pier searching for the woman.

The first police car took fifteen minutes to arrive, it felt more like an hour. An officer asked for information, I pointed to the barge where she had so suddenly vanished.

'We have summoned a river police boat from Wapping that will search the area,' he said calmly. 'Cover the banks, she may have swum ashore,' he ordered four policemen. The barge lay near rocky beaches, only exposed along the banks at low tide, they were strewn with debris; save some ducks and a gaggle of geese foraging on the shore, nothing else stirred, there was certainly no sign of the young woman. I helplessly watched a small police boat circle the barge; alas officers on board reported nothing.

A chill wind blew across the Thames. Tired policemen had shaken their heads, having failed to find any trace of her. Flashing lights from their cars retreated into a side street. I stood alone feeling distraught, and gazed at the tide heaving past the barge. Tower Bridge's unmistakable outline emerged from the mist, a parade of restored warehouses and flats led towards Canary Wharf, hovering like a futuristic temple over East London; somewhere in this vast stretch of water lay that beautiful woman.

It was getting dark. Lights twinkled enticingly from the Angel pub overlooking the river. I strode along Bermondsey embankment and headed there. I needed a drink. The Angel was almost empty; as soon as I had walked through the door, the warmth and cosy feel to the place revived me a little. I carried my pint to a table near an elderly man smoking a pipe. Taking a long slurp I glanced out of a window at the river. I shuddered. The Thames had always seemed so alluring, now I resented it. The man had been examining me. He appeared like a caricature of an old sailor, a straggly, grey beard framed a broad, wrinkled face.
'You look like you've had a rough day,' he said. I nodded.
'I've had better.'
I'm a good listener,' he answered exhaling a puff of smoke. I shook my head.
'What if I said that I witnessed a young woman jump from a barge into the river, just off Bermondsey pier?'
'I see . . . did they find the body then?' the old sailor said rubbing his beard.
'No, they didn't.'
'That's no surprise,' he announced in a matter of fact way.
'What do you mean? I saw with my own eyes a woman jump. The police cam. I could do nothing.'
'Are you sure she jumped?'
'Yes!' I protested. 'She was on a barge right in front of me, then she disappeared.'
'Disappeared then . . .'
'Yes disappeared!'

'I know you are upset, as anybody would be in such circumstances, but there is a big difference between jump and disappear.'

'What are you trying to tell me? That I imagined the whole event? The police doubted me too.'

'Not exactly,' he said with a glint in his eye, 'but I will be surprised if they ever find her body.'

'Due to the river currents you mean, God knows where her body could have been swept to,' I moaned, picturing her slim figure entangled with refuse on the riverbed.

'I didn't say that.'

'What are you saying then?' I demanded, slamming my glass on the table.

'Well, let me tell you that I worked in Bermondsey docks for many years when it was still the Port of London. There is a legend that every so often an angel, the angel of Bermondsey, appears from the river. I saw her a couple of times - fleeting glimpses though, but I definitely saw her!'

'Are you saying that I'm seeing ghosts?'

'Maybe. The first time, I thought it was my bloody imagination, too much ale, but other dockers had sworn that they had glimpsed her too. She's not a ghost - an angel!'

'So where did this angel come from?' I asked, taking the conversation with a pinch of salt.

'Mmm . . .' he groaned and leant towards me, 'the story goes that a woman threw herself into the river when she found out her lover, a sailor, had died in a shipwreck. Her body was never found but it is said that her spirit lives on.'

'When did this happen?'

'I'm not sure really, but sometime early last century . . .' he broke off, I could see he was racking his brains. '1914!' he announced, 'that's it. The year the First World War started. It's amazing how you can remember such things, isn't it?'

'So when was the last time you saw this Angel?'

'Christ, I haven't seen her for at least forty years . . . ever since I stopped working on the river, she was so young, so beautiful, I still remember her smile.'

That night I had difficulty sleeping. Visions of the woman on the barge haunted me. It dawned on me that when she had jumped into the

Thames, there was no sound of a splash. The conversation with the old sailor played on my mind. 'The Angel of Bermondsey,' I muttered over and over again.

The next day I made some enquiries about where I could do some research. I discovered that a library in London stored newspapers in chronological order. Once at the library a miserable librarian escorted me to a CD Rom station where researchers could browse through published journals. At least I had a year to start from - 1914; nonetheless hundreds of papers are published in a year. I started in the January section and sifted through the month's news into February. It was like being transported back into history reading about events just reported; yet nothing on a drowned woman off Bermondsey materialised. From February to March - the sheer amount of information appearing on screen was overwhelming. I pessimistically searched through April, when I skimmed over a short article, so insignificant in size I almost overlooked it. 'Woman Drowns in Thames', it read. The date was right - 1914. The article stated a 24 year old Lucinda Harthing, recently widowed following the death of her husband Edward Harthing, had drowned in the river off Bermondsey Pier . . . her body was never retrieved. My heard pounded hard, I had discovered the needle in the haystack mountain. 'Lucinda Harthing!' I gasped rereading the article over and over again.

I returned to Bermondsey pier that afternoon, images of the beautiful woman on the barge were now stamped in my mind with the newspaper article from 1914. It all seemed ridiculous, but something drove me back there, to the spot where I saw her jump into the Thames. I walked down the pier, the barge, now so ingrained in my memory appeared at its mooring . . . the barge was empty. Bathed in evening sunlight the Thames sparkled, never had it looked so serene. I waited, foolishly expecting to see an angel. Was this insanity? I looked at my watch, it was approaching six o'clock. A churning boat engine was getting louder, and louder behind me. A female figure emerged on the barge, she mesmerised me with that unforgettable smile, and it seems she was expecting me. She waved at something in the river; I turned and saw an approaching boat. It was the same boat that had passed us the day before. I read her name painted in black letters along the sleek hull - *The Lucinda*. I glanced back at the barge. She was gone. Only then did I notice an advertising panel on the barge's deck where she was standing; it read 'Edward and Son Freight Ltd'. The Lucinda surged by. V-shaped swell trailing the boat shone a dazzling gold as it spread out and lapped against the barge; for a fleeting moment a connection seemed to be made between the two vessels. As The Lucinda cruised towards Tower Bridge and the shimmering skyline of the City beyond, I stood on the pier watching her form disappear into the evening glow. Stillness returned to the river at Bermondsey pier, the barge moaned softly. I heard laughter coming from a pub on the bank from the Angel.

DON'T JUDGE A BOOK BY ITS COVER
Karen Churchward

The first on the moon structures went up in 2045. It was a small space observatory, as an experiment. During the second and third decades of the twenty-first century, as space observation became increasingly more important and telescopes more sophisticated, the biggest problems the astronomers faced was weather restrictions. It was during an informal delay meeting that the notion of an observatory on the moon was first joked about. However, one of them kept the idea mulling over in his head and brought it up in the next meeting. An observatory where weather conditions could never interfere with their viewings and computers could be let to run them with minimal human interference. It was an excellent idea - to build one outside the Earth's atmosphere. So the first of the moon structures was built in 2045. The first anomaly was found two years later, in 2047.

The small observatory was a complete success. It easily withstood the small pieces of flying debris that bounced up from the moon's surface from time to time and, with the obvious absence of air and water, there was no other threat to the building from the elements. Even when the trip to the moon was included, the cost of building it was much smaller than if it had been built on Earth as much thinner, lighter materials, could be used and so the construction of a much larger observatory was soon underway.

One of the construction workers was digging through the rock to lay the foundations. He had to dig much deeper than they did for the smaller tower and he'd gone down about 50 feet when his Electromagnetic Signal Indicator's reading changed. Its reading started to increase as he was digging and by 55 feet it had increased dramatically. The digger also felt the rock was easier to dig through. It seemed more like compact dust than solid rock. He was just thinking about whether he should tell someone about the rock getting thinner, as he was concerned about the foundation strength, when he got thrown slightly backwards as he hit something really hard. The digger regained his balance and tried to dig again. This time he was prepared so put a bit of extra force behind the drill, but could not penetrate the rock. He had a couple more attempts when he remembered the Electromagnetic Indicator and again checked its reading. As the reading suggested such a magnetic force was below that it could only mean a large area of magnetic material, he decided it was time to tell somebody.

The suspicions were soon confirmed that the digger had, in fact, discovered an area of solid metal as the team dug away around the hole to find its edge. The whole operation was done in silence. It was the kind of uncomfortable silence when you all know something is very wrong yet nobody wants to be the first to point it out. They all knew there was every possibility there would be traces of metal naturally within the moon rock, but as they dug across the surface of the find they soon realised the size of the metal area discovered was far too large to be natural.

Eight hours later an area of metal estimated to be about 2 metres thick was uncovered measuring approximately 3 kilometres square and a meeting was called on Earth. It was first and foremost decided that the crew on the moon were to immediately leave their posts and return back to the planet. The crew currently on the moon were simply construction workers with just one qualified astronaut and a specialist team needed to be put together to investigate further. It was also decided that the discovery on the moon would be kept a secret for the time being until they knew what they were dealing with. The construction crew arrived back on Earth 24 hours later and were immediately taken to a secure unit within the NASA site where they were referred to the section of their contracts covering the events in a security situation. They were told they were to remain at NASA until further notice and their families were to be told they were still on the moon. They were assured they were not prisoners, however, breaches of their contracts would result in them being detained, so were all asked for their co-operation in this matter until further notice.

A specialist crew consisting of military experienced astronauts left for the moon later that day, carrying much more sophisticated digging equipment and measuring instruments. They followed their instructions upon arrival at the new discovery and drilled a small hole through the metal until it bored through to the other side. They then waited. They waited for almost an hour at a distance, again in the same uncomfortable silence, constantly measuring noise and gas emission.

The air from the other side of the hole quickly escaped and they measured it as similar to that on Earth but with a much lower level of oxygen - too low for a human to breathe. However it confirmed there was an artificial atmosphere created within the core of the moon that caused the moon crew and the whole of the control room at NASA to wait in anxious anticipation for a reaction. They now had to explore the possibility that the atmosphere created within the discovery could have been created for other intelligent life and the chamber, which had now obviously been built, could actually have alien life in it. The instruments also picked up a very, very slight noise vibration. It was so slight it barely registered, but it was constant so it was easy to confirm it was there. However, as there was no other activity whatsoever, and no motion or communication type sound wave had been detected the crew returned to the chamber, as they decided it was. Two of them bore a much large hole through the metal, another two measured for any changes in the vibration or atmosphere, two stood waiting with their laser guns poised at the hole that was being created, while the remaining two members of the crew sat back at the lunar module in case a quick get away was required. The hole was created without any other activity and the large square of metal was gently eased out to reveal a dark, black hole. Flashlights revealed much the same and failed to penetrate the light enough to see very far into the immense blackness below and so they sent down a flare. They lay across the metal surface and peered down into the hole, each with a camera as they waited for the flare to ignite fully. On the count of 15 the flare lit up a large area of the hole. It was a much deeper chamber than they'd anticipated, but they could still faintly see its base. They all took as many Polaroid's as they could, of all angles. They only had about a minute before the flare burnt itself out and they needed all the information they could get as to what they were dealing with. They soon realised the chamber was one huge room which measured approximately 4 kilometres cubed. All the walls appeared solid so there were no other corridors or chambers hiding more unknown phenomena for them to worry about. They also soon realised the faint hum was caused by machinery working, as limited as it was. Most importantly, though, they discovered there was no other life present, alive or dead, as was first feared. There was just some equipment that had been put there within our moon by a race completely unknown to us. For the first time mankind was physically looking at evidence of other life in our universe.

From their findings the crew proceeded down into the chamber. After all the excitement and anticipation they found themselves slightly disappointed at the minimal operation the aliens had set up, yet as the initial disappointment passed, they each realised they were actually relied that they didn't find anything too unknown or dangerous. There was a central column with a suspended spinning ball on it, which was where the low humming noise was coming from. Along one wall were 10 much thinner columns, each with a small cylinder on the top and that was it. The captain of the crew approached one of the cylinders and tapped it. They were all made of metal and each shone in their flashlights, completely free of any erosion or tarnish. The part facing the wall appeared to be made of layered glass. On closer inspection he realised they appeared to be lenses. He then went back to the centrepiece of the room. A perfect ball approximately 30cm in diameter was spinning slowly, suspended just a few millimetres from the tapered column rising from the floor. He walked around it several times, trying to decide on his next move. He nodded towards one of the armed crew, who pointed his laser at the ball and when he was covered in the event of a reaction, he put out his gloved hand and very gently touched the ball. It moved very, very slightly, yet an invisible force bought it back into line almost immediately. Nothing else happened for a few more gentle pushes, so the astronaut tried to lift it away. Although it did not appear to be connected in any way to the column he could lift it no more than a few more millimetres, so he decided to push it down. It pushed into the top of the column with complete ease and they stood there for almost a minute assuming nothing had happened again. They were anticipating their next move when one of the armed men moved his gun towards one of the walls, quickly followed by the other armed man and with a second a half they were all staring in disbelief at a completely transparent wall. The plain metal that was there before was no longer visible and in its place was a window that allowed them to stare directly into space. The initial shock at the sudden change deepened as they all acknowledged they were staring at the Earth. The side had become transparent was the one with the columns, which it now seemed were staring directly at the planet. Already with their senses alert, they immediately noticed when the humming tone changed. The captain of the mission moved the men out straight away. He decided too many changes in the already strange environment were occurring. They left the site and returned to the shuttle for immediate take-off and the headquarters back on Earth made the decision to quarantine the moon until further notice.

The final change completed within the chamber. In one of the corners a large circular area had materialised, filled with white, wispy smoke. As the shuttle sped away from the moon the men inside were never to know they could have witness the first gateway into another civilisation that would, for now, remain unbeknown to us.

TONSILLITIS AND TREACLE
Yvonne Granger

The doctor called on a winter's day in 1965, he had become a frequent visitor during my recurring bouts of tonsillitis. His verdict was disappointing, no return to school yet, I must continue to rest and try to eat a little more to build up my strength.

The front room, which was only used on high days and holidays, had been made into a makeshift sickroom, to isolate me from my two sisters and any visitors who might call. It was an expensive and exciting luxury to have a roaring fire lit, just for me, during my convalescence, but the novelty had worn thin and even the cat, my constant and only companion, had now deserted the fireside for a forage out of doors. Mum popped in and out to check on me throughout the day, but her chores around the house meant I was left for what seemed an eternity, to entertain myself. Daytime television was fifteen years away and 'Listen With Mother' and 'Woman's Hour' on the bakelite radio, did little to stimulate the mind of a nine-year old.

It was normal for only the back room to be used, it served as kitchen, dining and sitting room, depending on the time of day. There was no electric immersion heater, so the fire had to be kept in both day and night, making it the only room with constant heating in our small council house. The last task each evening would be to put coal dust and ash onto the fire to allow it to smoulder through the night. The back boiler provided the only hot water and baths had to be shallow and shared. When my sisters and I were younger, the old stone kitchen sink had been big enough for us to be bathed in, but as we outgrew it, we had to make do with a few inches of hot water in the bath. We were all washed together and quickly towelled down, in the unheated bathroom, just before Dad returned home from his shift on the buses. He would then top up the water and take a more leisurely soak.

Hot water, being the precious commodity it was, meant the family wash was a weekly event which took place each Monday. Mum would disappear into the shed for the day, where she would light the gas boiler under the 'copper', which was a huge wrought iron tub which bubbled and hissed as the water heated. Billowing steam would emanate from the windows and door, as she agitated the linen with her wooden 'copper' stick, lifting the gloriously aromatic washing out and feeding it through the hand-operated mangle, before hanging the snowy white linen, still steaming, onto the washing line. There, with the clothes prop lifting the line high, the sheets would catch the wind, like the sails of a cutter crossing the ocean. There has never been a washing machine manufactured, that could emulate the whites which Mum produced from that old copper!

Salvation from my boredom, came in the form of our next-door neighbour, who left me some old hardback books to read. I had never really been a bookworm, although Mum had always read aloud to my sisters and I, especially at bedtime. It was usually Enid Blyton's tales of fairies and goblins, which lulled us to sleep, as was the intention, but during the next few days in my sickbed, I read Black Beauty and National Velvet, books which inspired and enthralled me and led me to discover a whole new world of places and people which provided the stimulus which led me, in later life, to become a voracious reader.

After a few days of reading, resting and eating more substantially, my spirits and health perked up and I was allowed into the garden for some fresh, or one might call it, bracing air. There was little risk of catching a chill however, dressed as I was in my rubber-buttoned liberty bodice, jumper and cardigan, pixie bonnet and scarf, all hand knitted by Mum, plus the essential fashion item of the day, mittens on a piece of elastic, threaded through my coat sleeves for safe keeping! Suitably attired, I was allowed out into the garden, whilst Mum hung the washing out, it was so cold the linen froze as stiff as a board, almost as soon as she pegged it on the line.

'We need a sharp frost to kill off the germs,' was a popular philosophy of the day and is probably why the mortality rate amongst children was much higher in the sixties! Nevertheless, I roamed about the garden stamping in frozen puddles and breaking icicles off the bird bath, quite enjoying my taste of freedom, despite the biting cold.

Whilst Mum continued her fight against the elements, I wandered around to the front garden to swing on the gate and see if anybody was about in the road. The bleak weather seemed to have encouraged people to stay indoors, the smoking chimneys, evidence that everyone had their fires well stoked against the cold. The house at the end of the terrace opposite, had new occupants, I had seen them arrive the previous day, in a large van which had delivered both family and furniture to the house. Mum had scolded me for pulling the curtains right back for a better view, not wishing to give the impression we were nosy neighbours, but I had, by that time, managed to establish that they were an elderly couple and they had a dog!

From my perch on the gate, I could see the dog in the garden opposite and despite Mum's warning not to roam, my curiosity got the better of me. I hopped down and ran across to peep cautiously over the privet hedge. By the time I went back home, a quarter of an hour later, I had introduced myself to the lady who had moved in and questioned her exhaustively about her pet.

Being only nine had its advantages, you could ask anything you like and not have to worry about snooping!

The weather improved slightly and whilst my sisters and all the other children from the street were at school, I was allowed to spend longer periods out of doors to aid my recovery. The doctor visited again and was pleased with my improved pallor and encouraged me to take in as much fresh air as possible. This allowed me to spend lots of my time with my new canine friend, Treacle, who, I was informed, was a pedigree golden retriever. He would lay looking out of the gate until he caught sight off me crossing the road, then his tail would wag and he seemed to mark time on the spot until I arrived. He would follow me up and down his side of the privet hedge, as I rode my scooter back and forth on the pavement. He loved to have his head stroked and he became my friend and confidant during an extremely lonely time in my young life.

Ironically, I was allowed back to school, a week before the break for Christmas, which was probably not a bad thing, as I was still weaker than I realised, but I would be able to attend the school party and carol service.

School was only a ten minute walk away, down a muddy lane and my sisters and I, together with a host of other children from our road, would set off at around half-past eight, dawdling into school just before the nine o'clock registration bell. There was so much to see and do on that short walk, it was quite an adventure in itself. The lane had a copse of trees and a field on one side and a few old cottages on the other. One particular dwelling was rather a ramshackle affair and widely reputed to be haunted, the lurid invention of one of the older boys, but everyone, including them, still hurried past it just in case!

There were no paths to walk on and when it rained, there would be enormous puddles to leap, splash and play dare in. During the winter it provided a wonderful frozen area to slide and skid on and I do not suppose there was a single child walking that route, who paid the slightest heed to their parents' warnings not to play in the puddles, climb the trees or go on the ice, it was an irresistible temptation! The hedgerows were full of blossoms in the spring and hips and haws in the winter, there was always something to take to school for the nature table. There was even a murky stream, where the more daring could find tadpoles and frog spawn and even an occasional stickleback!

Despite being amongst my friends once more, I never let a day go by without saying hello to Treacle, who would wait patiently at the gate each morning and afternoon to be patted and stroked, by the steady stream of youngsters going to, or returning from school. It has always intrigued me that even our cat was aware of school times and made sure he was in his position on the gatepost to maximise his chances of being petted.

Christmas came and went and was followed by several weeks of heavy snow, the like of which we have not seen since. It had little effect on day to day life, however, and did not bring the country to a standstill, as a sprinkling is inclined to do nowadays. The traffic on the roads was minimal and folk seemed ever resourceful in overcoming the conditions. As children we never had a splendid wooden sledge, but we were blessed with an inventive Dad and spent many happy hours at the old sandpit, sliding down the slopes in an old tin bath which, unlike its wooden counterpart, could accommodate both myself and my sisters.

My health improved by leaps and bounds that spring and in hindsight, I can see that my time at home that winter, proved useful in shaping many aspects of my life.

I have learnt much more from the books read over the years, than I ever did at school and I did, eventually, when I was grown, get to have a dog of my own. He is every inch the companion that Treacle was and he and I regularly visit Mum and Dad in that same little house. They own it now, something they would have laughed at, had it been suggested during those lean times. As a family, we had no money to spare, but in terms of happiness and love, I know we were rich beyond compare.

Strangely, my normally obedient dog, refuses to depart my parents' house, until we cross the road to the garden wall which replaced the old privet hedge. He looks over into the garden and observes something which I can no longer perceive. He is drawn to that place, as I had been so many years before. Perhaps that unfathomable sixth sense, which animals undeniably possess, permits him to catch sight of my old acquaintance, Treacle, still keeping his daily vigil by the gate?

JEREMIAH'S TEAR
Stephen Ralph

Jeremiah was a tree of a man. Big, strong and stout like an oak. His hands were gnarled, his skin a tree's bark, his hair wild yet beautifully unkempt. People carved their names into his thighs and he did not complain. His wife chiselled a heart upon his chest and the heart circled each of their initials so as she was in his heart every day.

Jeremiah stood strong and solid in the most terrifying storms, the driest heat, the starchest summers and unrelenting winters of torrential rain, giving hope and reassurance to everyone in the village below. Looking out from their windows in the most stormy of nights or peaceful of evenings, they would see Jeremiah standing tall and dependable upon his mountain, his roots steadfast and immovable. A beacon in a storm. A sure light in the shadows.

He saw it all come and go and still he stood there on his mountain taking in all the changes of the world. Every generation. Wise to their innocence and wonder. Never complaining, never passing unwanted opinion. He would not judge their ignorance and stubborn pig-headedness. He tolerated their brutality and warmed at their brotherhood. Jeremiah saw it all with the serene wisdom of the tree that he was.

And so the heavens opened when he wept and his tears threatened to flood the village, such was his grief when his beautiful wife passed away. But the villagers did not mind and they came to watch the great man sob, standing vigil as he cried his ocean of tears, their livelihoods swamped by his overwhelming emotion and they did not begrudge him his sadness. Jeremiah wept for twelve years and twenty-eight days and in respect for the man the sky remained overcast and the sun refused to shine.

When he'd done crying, Jeremiah raised his head and viewed the waterlogged valley. The water subsided and an oasis of colour and beauty had grown beneath its ebb tide. Flowers stood as tall as trees. People had never seen so many variations of green. A rainbow of foliage decorated the valley as far as the eye could see and the villagers flocked to thank the wise, old tree of a man on the mountainside and no one begrudged Jeremiah his grief. The sun gave him a knowing nod and the grey rain clouds bid him a loving farewell.

Jeremiah clasped his huge hands together and sobbed his final sob. A lone tear of wonder at the beauty of his sorrow skied over the bridge of his nose, down his wind-beaten cheek, over his lips and free-fell from his chin onto the lush mountainside grass, becoming the envy of the dew as it rolled between the jungle of grass, a myriad of beautiful colour reflecting and sparkling off it in shards of sunlight as it made its way down to the mountain beck.

Jeremiah's tear launched fearlessly into the icy cold water and lay on its back, swept along by the current of the mountain stream, bathing in happiness and the warmth of beauty. Everyone gawped in awe of Jeremiah's final tear as it swept downstream.

Parades were held to coincide with its passing through. Schools were given holidays, the banks remained shut and hostelries open as everyone celebrated Jeremiah's wonderful tear. People flanked the banks and held carnivals and street parties as it floated through other villages and towns, along canals and waterways where the rats bowed and the swans curtseyed at its brilliance for surely it was the most beautiful tear to behold.

Jeremiah's final tear eventually made it to the sea where passing tankers steered well around it and fish jumped to be in its presence. And the Lord saw its beauty and marvelled.

The tear floated up to the skies glistening in the azure heavens, dazzling passing aircraft and making gulls swoop and holler with joy. And the Lord froze Jeremiah's tear as a monument to man's strength, weakness, sorrow and joy, creating a silver cloud of the softest eider and silk especially for the tear.

And only the most crystal sky housed the cloud and the cloud held the tear and together they travelled the world decorating childhood summers of abandon and smiles, holiday photographs of squinting families, village fetes and country weddings. The cloud created first loves, sheltered injured animals, inspired painters' imaginations and coloured their easels. And the years passed, the decades and the centuries and the cloud preserved Jeremiah's tear in all its original glory.

The story of Jeremiah's tear passed down from generation to generation. The horse told the foal, the cow told the calf, the wind told the grass and the mountains told the sea. Each new summer heard from the dying embers of spring and passed on the message to autumn and in winter the glint from Jeremiah's frozen tear, nestled in the luxury of the cloud, made the deaf hear its beauty and the blind see it.

The Old Man of Oban heard the story in this way. One fantastically cold spring day, as a weak and weary fly relented itself to its final breaths, snared in the trap of his sugar-spun web, it relayed to him the story it had heard as a blind and fretful maggot, of Jeremiah's tear, the most perfect specimen of human strength and weakness, preserved in a silken cloud too perfect even for heaven.

The Old Man had thanked his prey for the passing on of the story and had dreamt of the tear ever since, in turn relaying the tale to fellow spiders and insect creatures of his acquaintance.

A tugboat had taken him to the mainland, a bird had flown him to the glens. As he quaked under foot of farm hands and ramblers, bathed in the glory of a blackberry patch in a stifling summer's heat or floated downstream on a raft of fallen leaves he had visioned Jeremiah's tear in all is startling precision.

And now he was old. His beard marked the passing of time and the hairs on his legs were no longer adequate protection against the bleak winter winds of the north. That day he had relentlessly battled the wind and sewn himself a web with which to shut out the ice in the air, all the time dreaming of the beauty of Jeremiah's tear. And now his toil was done and he shivered inside his silver bivouac, fleeting memories of his life's journey returning to haunt and humour him.

The Old Man was feeling very old. Older than he had ever felt before. His days were coming to an end and soon the Lord would claim his soul and it too would join all other dead souls becoming part of the icy winter's breeze, wafting in, out, over and under people's lives, just his bones and his body left here in his sleeping bag of a web for someone to find and dust away. And as a cloud passed overhead, he found himself once again thinking of Jeremiah's tear and how he envied it preserved and everlasting.

The cloud hovered above. Jeremiah's tear felt no fear or regret. It looked down upon creation and yearned for its uncertainty. Something inside told it this was the right decision to make. The cloud began sobbing but knew that the tear was doing the right thing and as the sun lit up all the deficiencies and dreams of man, woman, child and every living, breathing creature below the tear free-fell to the ground laughing with eyes wide open.

The Old Man of Oban huddled in the shelter of his web and not for the first time cried for the beauty of Jeremiah's story. A single, solitary spider's tear escaped his web and joined the glistening raindrops on the window, cutting its own path through the spaghetti of condensation that raced to bathe in the oily puddles on the sill.

Jeremiah's tear hit the window at approximately the same time and too began crossing the myriad rivulets towards the gravitational pull of the forming puddles, dancing with a rainbow-like spectrum of colours.

Criss-crossing the windowpane, ducking, bobbing and weaving their separate journeys south, the two tears unknowingly ventured closer and closer until a collision course was set and the two veered directly into each other, dropping like mercury, each gaining momentum from the other and plummeting faster and faster until they eventually cascaded into the oily pools on the window sill, splashing and revelling in each other's company with gay abandon and disregard for consequence, for this was meant to be.

They sang Irish folk songs and ancient sea shanties in foreign tongues neither had ever known before. Their pleasure belied fate, time, religion, distance, age, sex, race, colour, class and every other help or hindrance civilisation had created. The two tears submerged themselves in the gaiety of the moment and the surety of themselves. They paddled, dive-bombed, floated and splashed and the Lord looked on and was momentarily infected by their contagious and brilliant bright light. A light seen by the ghosts of suicides who immediately understood.

The light shone so brightly whilst it lasted and when the weather changed, the puddles dried and the passing souls in the icy wind ceased their grieving wails and the moment was gone, I still basked in the memory of the glory of what I witnessed on my window sill that very day.

So like the fly to the Old Man of Oban and the dusk to the dawn. Like a father to a son I now pass the story on to you. The story of Jeremiah's tear. And if you are the type of person who looks up to admire the architecture of the world around you as you pass through it, rather than dwelling on the cracks and deficiencies at street level, then you too might one day collide with a bright light and amidst the momentary pain and shock of impact, swoon in all its wonderful colour.

And if at that moment you remember the story of Jeremiah's tear then please pass it on.

THE TWINS, A TRUE STORY
Elisabeth D Perrin

Can you sit a while and listen to my story? It's about a family called James.

Mr and Mrs James had a family of six daughters, the youngest of which were twins. They lived in a pleasant house with a beautiful garden, in a small country village with fields, trees and an area of woods as far as the eye could see. The name of the village was Penault, situated a few miles from the historic town of Monmouth. The daughters were Mary, Hanna, Elisabeth, Jessica and the twins, Suzanna and Harriet, who were the youngest.

Mary went to work on a nearby farm, as she always loved animals. Hanna was a very good cook and she became head cook for a well-to-do family. Elisabeth decided to stay at home and Jessica met a wealthy man on a visit to Monmouth and they eventually married, moved to Newport, set up in business investing in a small hotel.

But a strange thing happened to the twin sisters. Let me explain! One day, a few of the village folk noticed to their dismay that three gypsy caravans had camped by the edge of the woods. The first person to see them was in fact the local woodcutter, who was working in the woods at the time cutting logs. Word soon got around the village and parents decided to stop their young children from visiting or playing in or near the woods. The children were, of course, quite unhappy about this and so was in fact the old woodcutter as he missed the children coming along and chattering to him, as he was always on his own and the woods were so quiet, except for birds and other wildlife. He therefore hoped that the gypsies would not stay for long, both for his own sake and that of the village folk and he had even considered asking the local policeman if they could be moved along.

Now Suzanna, being a young, pretty girl of eighteen, was very curious to see what the gypsies were like and after hearing different stories from her friends became even more interested. So just after teatime one warm summer's day, she decided to go for a walk on her own and visit the woods. Her mother and father asked where she was going, especially on her own, she'd said, 'Only for a short walk.' They told her not to be long and be back before it started to get dark and on no account to go near the woods.

In the meantime, the caravans were getting ready to leave because of the hostility of the village people towards the gypsies, as no one wanted them setting up camp in the village.

Meanwhile back at the house, Mr and Mrs James were helping Harriet to prepare to leave in the morning on a long sea journey by sailing ship for New Zealand, having been engaged as a nanny to a wealthy family living nearby. They had two children, a boy of four and a girl of six, and were leaving to live in New Zealand. They were very fond of Harriet and treated her as one of their own family, so when one day they asked her if she would like to travel with them, she gave it some thought and finally agreed. Thinking of the long journey ahead and the thought of leaving her family behind Harriet retired to bed, unaware of the trouble that was ahead for her mother and father.

Meanwhile, Mr and Mrs James became increasingly worried about Suzanna and prayed she had not gone to the woods where the gypsies were camped. Mr James set off in search of his daughter looking everywhere, moving his lantern here and there while walking through the woods. He was also quite surprised and thought it odd that suddenly the gypsies had gone. They seemed to have completely disappeared and no one was in sight, he thought how glad he was that they had gone. He continued to search, but to no avail and decided he would have to report his missing daughter to the police.

A search was organised but no trace was ever found of poor Suzanna. Later, other police were called on to help, but no trace was ever found of her and eventually, the file was put aside as they began to suspect that the gypsies may have lured her away with them when they left. No one ever knew if she had put up a fight trying to get away, or if she had been kidnapped. Suzanna was never seen again, she had been lost forever, their beautiful daughter.

Harriet in the meantime knew nothing of this as the news was kept from her. They even lied to her about her sister, telling her not to worry as she was still fast asleep, so Harriet said her goodbyes and departed early in the morning. Many weeks went by before a letter arrived from

Harriet to say she had reached Wellington, New Zealand, after a long and stormy voyage during which time she had been seasick and still felt poorly, even after some time on land. The letter described her new home and how beautiful it was and she asked about Suzanna and longed for a letter from her.

Mr and Mrs James were trying to get on with their lives, taking each day at a time, but things were not the same, their minds were filled with thoughts of the twins and how their lives had turned out, it was a sad time for them. Mrs James felt guilty that she had lied to Harriet each time she had written about Suzanna, knowing how homesick she was feeling. Harriet even sent a special letter pleading with her mother to tell Suzanna to write a few lines as she had much to tell her sister. So Mrs James decided to sit down and write to tell Harriet the bad news about her sister. As she began to write, she became heartbroken and decided to leave it for another day, as she knew Harriet would be upset so far away from home.

The time had gone so fast, soon a year had passed and Mrs James began to feel poorly, especially with another winter approaching. Then one day as she was feeling particularly low, a letter arrived from New Zealand which really brightened up her spirits. Her daughter had met a very nice man called Charles. He was a qualified doctor, quite a few years older than her, but very kind. Mrs James did not mind this as her eldest daughter Hanna had married a man ten years older than her. Harriet said they had become engaged and informed Mrs James that a date for the wedding would be set later, perhaps even in a few months. 'How wonderful,' thought Mrs James, 'I'm so happy for her, but will I ever see her again?'

As the weeks went by, Mrs James' health became increasingly worse and she became quite ill, getting weaker day by day, and her daughter Elisabeth was worried that she would not be able to cope much longer. Eventually, the local doctor was sent for, but there did not seem much hope. some days she would ask if there was any news, or if there was a letter from Harriet and even mentioned dear Suzanna, even though she had long since disappeared.

Elisabeth decided to send for her sister Hannah, who was married to a farmer and lived a few miles away. She had three children, two boys and a girl, but she came at once, the children being kept away from the sickbed. One of her neighbours offered to look after the children, as they had a big house and had children of their own.

Within weeks, Mrs James had passed away and they tried to get news to Harriet as quickly as possible. The weeks went by, but still no news from Harriet. They could not understand the reason for such a long delay and thought maybe she had got married and had moved. They did not know what to think. Then one day a letter finally arrived, and what a heartbreaking letter it was for all the family. Harriet had become ill and the doctor she was engaged to was with her every day. She knew she was fading away and longed to come home, as she wished to die at home, but she was too ill to face the long sea journey to England. Of course, the wedding had been postponed, but Charles kept true to Harriet to the end and she died in his arms, thousands of miles from the rest of her family.

What with all his terrible losses, Mr James was grieving every day and could not come to terms with the loss of his dear wife and his daughter. He became quite ill and died, many said from a broken heart. The house was sold up and the family went their different ways.

Months passed, when Hanna received a lovely letter from Charles in New Zealand saying that he had arranged everything for dear Harriet and that she was buried in a cemetery at Wellington, not far from his home. He said he was able to walk to the grave and take flowers each week, he also said he would be shipping over a large trunk with all Harriet's belongings and her wedding trousseau. A few months later the trunk arrived. Hanna was unable to bring herself to open it up for a week, but what a surprise when she did. Such beautiful gowns, all neatly packed, rings and other lovely jewellery. 'She always did look smart,' Hannah thought, with tears coming to her eyes. 'Now I'll have to get on with my life,' she said, 'no longer have I got twin sisters.'

The Frightened Man
A R Bell

Robert sat quietly, his hands on the steering wheel of his car. A restless man, who two months before had won a small fortune, £12,000 on the football pools. The year was 1960 and the spring flowers were bursting into life as he passed through the countryside.

Always a loner, a thinker, a silent 'plotter' with no close friends. At thirty years old, he had lost his parents in an accident ten years ago, perhaps this explained his attitude.

He was driving aimlessly looking for property he might be interested in - living in lodgings, he was responsible to nobody, so he pleased himself.

Suddenly he braked and the car came to a halt. A notice read, 'For Sale', this applied to half an acre of land and an old, rundown building. Robert got out of the car, locked the doors and clambered over the fence which surrounded the property. He walked over to the rundown ruins, he frowned as he saw the state of them. 'Don't look good!' he said loudly. He stumbled over scattered bricks as he mused, ' I wonder what they are asking for this old rubbish?' Three old oak trees almost surrounded the ruins. 'God!' said Robert aloud, 'These ruins must be ancient, but the land is OK.' His curiosity made him continue his search as he approached the giant oak trees, he stumbled over something hidden by the tall weeds. He swore as he got to his feet. 'What the hell was that?' He searched, then saw a large iron ring, rusted over. He pulled hard on the ring but it didn't budge. Then he got a fallen branch from a tree and, placing it through the ring, he levered it back and forth until a great groan lifted it and revealed a wooden opening. Robert stood there transfixed, as before him was a cellar full of weird damp smells. He looked around to see if he could be seen from the road. He was satisfied that he was not to be seen, being almost hidden by the ruins and trees.

Robert stood there for a full five minutes before lowering himself into the darkness of the hole, which he estimated was about eight foot deep. Robert struck a match and he almost fainted at what the light showed. A skeleton 'leaned' over a rough wooden bench, bony fingers on an old wooden box.

Almost a box of matches was used whilst Robert explored the cellar. Robert shuddered as he took the box from the bony fingers. With shaking hands he opened it. What he saw almost killed him with wonder. Precious gems filtered through his fingers as he lifted them from their hiding place. Robert stayed almost half an hour, then for some reason, took only half a dozen of the gems. Placing them in his pocket, he awkwardly climbed out of the cellar. His mind was in deep, dark thoughts. He carefully replaced the 'door' with the ring back in its place. He looked around and carefully moved out of the field and walked back to his car.

The week that followed was a busy one. Robert had to satisfy the agents that he and a group were interested in the old property and could they 'hold on' for three months. At a good profit, this was agreed and the 'For Sale' boards were removed. 'Three months,' said Robert to himself, 'I will have to be careful.'

The next day saw Robert in London carefully surveying the jewellery scene. The 'seedy', no questions asked places. The negotiations were completed in dark, threatening places and Robert received a third of the value of the gems. He was told not to talk, after Robert had promised further trade.

Robert returned to his lodgings and for the next few days was quiet with his thoughts. Strangely, he was becoming a more 'nervous' man, looking around furtively and questioning his actions. 'I've got three months to clear this lot up, then I can relax,' he spoke aloud. The next day, Robert drove to the property.

He parked his car carefully, then looking around nervously, he climbed over the hedge then to the ruins. His hands trembling violently, he took hold of the branch, inserted it into the ring and lifted the cover and lowered himself into the darkness. This time he brought a powerful torch and was able to take in the picture. Shaking with nerves and terror, he tripped and fell into the skeleton whose bones splintered at the impact. Robert let out a scream and he grabbed some jewellery and almost leaped out of the hole. He quickly replaced the cover and sat there in the weeds sobbing. After a while, he recovered and after glancing around him, he quickly left.

Robert was becoming a nervous wreck, his sleep was disturbed by skeletons and dark holes. He had been to London on three occasions and had sold quite a lot of the gems for which he had been paid one hundred thousand pounds. Robert was sure that he was being followed. Wealth was doing him no good. His body was crumbling, his hair grey and eyes bulging.

He wasn't wrong about his thoughts of being followed, for on his last trip to London, and after being paid, he saw other payments to a vicious-looking thug who was giving threatening glances towards him. After leaving London, he took several detours before driving home. Satisfied that he had outwitted the 'thug', he entered his room and removed a couple of floorboards. Taking out a large box, he added his last payment to the already huge some of banknotes, the box and floorboards were then replaced. Weariness overtook him and he lay fully dressed on the bed. Sleep would not come and his restless body tossed and turned. 'Have I done this and that? Have I been followed? Have I? Should I?' Suddenly a noise at the window brought him out of his questioning. He leaned under his bed and pulled out an axe which had been there since his nervous attacks. He had not switched on the light since returning home, so he silently slid from the bed and stood by the window. He watched, shaking, as he saw a bundle of rags was placed on the windowpane near the catch. Robert heard the crack as the revolver hit the rags. The splinters of glass landed at his feet as he stood there shaking. He then saw a hand on the catch. The window opened and a masked face peered in. In a flash, the axe in Robert's shaking hand flashed, the flat of the axe smashed into the head of the intruder, who was pulled into the room. Robert, hands shaking violently, took off the mask from the smashed head. It was the man who had been stalking him. All was quiet as the landlady was away at her daughter's for two days.

Robert stood shaking violently, not knowing what to do. It must have been fifteen minutes before he seemed to come out from a trance. Quickly he dragged the body from the house. Closing and locking the door behind him, Robert pulled the body to his car and bundled him into the boot. A crash of thunder added drama to the evening for it was quite dark. Robert knew exactly what was going to happen, in a strange way, his features lit up with excitement as the thunder and lightning split through the sky. In half an hour they arrived at the ruins. Robert got out of the car and almost ran to the boot to get rid of the body. He dragged it along the wet road and pulled it up and over into the field which was awash with rain. Thunder and lightning flashed all around them as Robert pulled and pushed the lifeless body to their destination. On reaching the ruins, Robert searched for the branch. This he found and it was used to lever the ring and board to reveal the interior of the cellar. With a cry of anger and madness, Robert heaved the body into the cellar. Then suddenly, his expression changed. 'He was meant to kill me, he got paid for it. I will have it.' Robert lowered himself into the hole which was now being illuminated and orchestrated by the heavens. He took a wad of notes from the body and decided to place the body beside the skeleton. By now the rain was beginning to flood the cellar so Robert decided to close the lid. Having done this, he sat the body of the gunman next to the skeleton.

He then stood pondering as if he had forgotten something. 'Ah!' he shouted, 'the gems! There must be some left, I'll take them!' As he struck the match to take the last of the treasure, a great flash of lightning, then a huge crash as one of the thirty ton trees crashed onto the cover, trapping those below.

A year has passed. Robert's car was found but with no trace of Robert. 'A very strange person, probably gone abroad,' was the conclusion.

MYRTLE'S SECRET
Phyllis Spooner

'It's crunch time now Myrtle,' she thought to herself as she faced Fred who lay motionless in front of her in the white hospital bed. 'Shall I tell him or not? And if I do, will it be for his sake or mine?' She peered at him. His face as white as the sheets, staring up at the lights. He had always stared like that when she spoke to him about something he didn't want to hear, thinking that if he didn't answer her the problem would go away. Now he was probably past caring about anything and she would be the one let with her secret on her conscience; and serve her right she supposed.

'Fred, would you like some water or fruit juice?' No reply. 'Well, if you want to doze, I'll go along to the canteen and I'll see you later. Alright?' Still no answer. He was happy staring at the lights. Maybe he would talk to the girls when they came in later.

Myrtle sat stirring her tea, she had also brought a wrapped sandwich which she really didn't want. It was in one of these plastic cases, hard to open. She'd no idea what was in it and she probably wouldn't eat it anyway. What was the time? Almost two o'clock. Susan, her eldest, would be along soon, but she would have to return home within the hour to pick up Barry from infant school.

'You'll wear a hole in that cup Mother.' Susan sat down. Myrtle drank her tea and Sue ate the sandwiches.
'How's Dad then?' She asked between mouthfuls.
'Much the same. Not saying a lot, but he looks comfortable.'
Myrtle knew that soon she would have to tell the children that she didn't think Fred would be coming home again. 'But how' she thought 'could she face telling them that?' Especially Angela, who was his favourite. Their son Edward would take it in his stride, she knew him well. He was like Fred. Didn't have a lot to say and was all for a quiet life. That was it. She'd had a boring life with Fred, though she shouldn't be thinking about that now, after all, he wasn't about to bore her for much longer. Suddenly tears ran down her cheeks. 'Oh Sue,' she said.
'Cheer up, Mum, maybe he will get better.' She waved as Angie came up to their table.

Myrtle glanced at Angie and as her daughter smiled at her, her heart missed a beat for it was once of those glances which took her back to the early days of her marriage, those happy days when life had not been boring. Life had never been boring during the three years that George Morgan had lodged with them. Even now she missed George. She missed his sense of humour, of which Fred had very little. She missed their chats. He did talk a lot but she loved his strong Welsh accent and she sometimes persuaded him to read to her from 'Under Milk Wood' when Fred was on late shift in the factory. They had become very close in no time and Susan, only a toddler when he arrived, loved him. Fred was awkward with the children; he seemed unable to climb down to their level to amuse them. she wondered so many times over the years whether George had ever married.

'Come on Mother,' called Sue. 'We're going to the ward now.'

As they walked in, the nurse was just drawing back the curtains from around Fred's bed. She said quietly to Myrtle, 'The doctor wants to have a chat with you before you go. Will your son be here later on?'

'Yes.'

'Good,' said the nurse abruptly, and strode off.

'How long can you stay Angie?' Myrtle began to worry that she would have to face the doctor alone if Edward was late.

'I can stay till five. I suppose I could come back in the evening if you want me.'

Myrtle was thankful that she had good, caring children. Her marriage had not been exactly joyous, but at least she would not be alone if Fred were to die. she looked down at Fred who was sleeping. She relived the early days of their marriage. When Susan was born they were so proud and happy but money was scarce and when Fred suggested that George might lodge with them for a short time, it seemed a good solution to their financial problems. And so it had been; but it had spelled disaster in another region.

'It was all your fault Fred,' Myrtle whispered aloud. Fred didn't stir. She didn't say she wished she'd never set eyes on George. After all, she had Angela, and whenever she studied her face or caught some of her mannerisms she could see there was no mistake. Angela was George's daughter. Not a soul knew about it, only Myrtle, and now she felt she must confess to Fred. She had deliberated about it these past few days and decided that he had a right to know that she had deceived him.

The girls had gone home and Edward had not yet arrived. Fred stirred and opened his eyes.
'Did you say something dear?'
'I said, Eddie will be here soon,' lied Myrtle.
'That's nice,' said Fred. 'When are the girls coming?'
'They've been here Fred, whilst you were sleeping.' Myrtle spoke kindly. She was so sorry for him. Maybe she shouldn't upset him today. He went off to sleep again.
'It was your fault Fred,' Myrtle whispered again. 'You worked long hours and left me with George. And one night you sent a message saying you were doing a full night-shift to fill in for someone, and George and I . . .well'
'Who are you talking to Mother? Dad's asleep.' Edward put his arm around her and said they had to see the doctor.
'So sorry Mrs Baker, we did our best . . .' Myrtle didn't catch everything he said, but Edward would tell her later.

When they returned to Fred's bedside he was awake and eager to chat. He asked Edward when he was going to marry Emma. Edward said 'soon' he thought.
'Good lad,' Fred looked happy.
'Just as he did on the night Edward was born,' thought Myrtle. He had wanted a son and he definitely was Fred's, she knew that. He looked like Fred then, and he still did. Pity Fred wouldn't see the wedding or any grandchildren bearing his name.

When Edward had gone home, Myrtle sat alone with Fred. The nurses had brought her food and given her a bed close by for the night. she had never felt so lonely, although she recalled how lonely she had been after George had gone. It had been a wonderful Christmas day. Edward was only ten months old but even he sensed it was a special day and George was so good with the girls whilst Myrtle cooked the turkey. She remembered how in one of his rare moments, Fred had gone upstairs to see to Edward when he cried. Probably because they'd all had a few drinks George became careless and that was when Fred caught them kissing in the sitting room.

'Get your coat and go,' thundered Fred.

'It was only a Christmas kiss Fred,' protested Myrtle.

But George went that night, and for a while, although she tried to cover it up, Myrtle felt that her heart was broken. They never saw George again.

Myrtle jumped. She had been dozing. Fred was talking.

'Myrtle, I've been meaning to ask you something for a long time, well, years really. I don't wish to upset you but I have to know.'

'Know what?'

'I want to know about one of the children, it's been on my mind for years.'

Myrtle tried to appear calm, but she was petrified. So Fred had beaten her to it. She should have confessed before.

'What is it then Fred?'

'It's Edward.'

'Edward? Edward did you say?' Myrtle was mystified now and more relaxed.

'Is Edward my son?'

'Is Edward your son? Of course he is. You can see that he is, surely? Oh Fred, what a question.'

'Swear that he is,' demanded Fred.

'Fred, I swear to you that Edward is your son.'

He closed his eyes and seemed at ease and content. He hadn't asked about Angie. And how could she tell him about her now? No, she would never confess to anyone. Also she knew that it would have to be her own dark secret; a great burden she would carry for the rest of her life.